OIL
ON MY
HANDS

A NOVEL 1 ERIC BONFIELD,
FROM THE FILES OF PRIVATE DETECTIVE-GEOLOGIST

BY: MAX REAMS

This book is a work of fiction. Names, characters, places, and incidents are the product of the author's imagination or are used fictitiously. Any resemblance to actual events, locations, or persons, living or dead, is coincidental.

Independently Published

Cover art by Randall Rupert and Gina M. Fiore

Chapter 1

"*A*re you certain your brother's death wasn't an accident or a suicide?" Sarah Isaacs glared at the private detective seated across her kitchen table. "Danny wouldn't kill himself!" she declared angrily. "Suicide is out of the question! And he was too careful to have an accident."

Eric Bonfield shifted uneasily in the straight-back kitchen chair. He feigned calm and tried to master his emotions. His mind whirled. *This is going nowhere. Better try another approach.*

"I'm sorry to ask these questions," he said, "but for me to help I need to dig as deep as I can into the situation."

Sarah took a deep breath, pushed a stray wisp of brown hair back, and exhaled slowly. She looked down at the kitchen table top, scratched by years of use, and tried to relax. "All right, I understand; you have to ask questions with obvious answers. At least the answers are obvious to me. I will try to be civil." She looked up and said, "I apologize for blasting you. These past days have been the worst in my life."

Eric nodded. "From what you've told me, this whole situation is horrendous. I really want to help." Sincerity showed in his well-sculptured face.

For the first time, Sarah looked directly into this man's blue, somewhat piercing eyes. They had a shimmering depth of pure beauty. Sarah stared in wonder. *Can a man's eyes be beautiful? This man sitting across from me does have beautiful eyes!* Embarrassed at her extended attention, she glanced to the side.

"Thanks for saying that. I'm hardly myself right now. Danny's death eats away at my heart." Tears trickled down her pretty, slender face.

Eric's professionalism melted, and compassion filled the wordless void between them. He wanted to do something to help her agitated state, but what? *If I reach across the table and take her hand, she might misinterpret my intentions. After all, I am a professional.* Eric's mind searched for what to do next. He lacked counseling skills, but he knew Sarah needed more than interrogation. At last he said, "This must be awful for you right now."

Sarah saw furrows of concern on his otherwise smooth brow. Her frustration began to ebb and her muscles relaxed. For the first time in days she sensed that somebody cared. A light smile crept across her well-formed lips. Finally she managed to say, "Thank . . . thank you."

Eric rose slowly from his chair. "Perhaps we ought to postpone our fact-finding session for a while. I can come back another time."

At this, Sarah snapped to attention. "Oh, no! I want to start this investigation right away. There's no time to lose. Something awful has happened, and the sooner we begin the better."

Caught half-way to a standing position, Eric reseated himself and took a notebook from his jacket pocket. Sarah noticed the title, *Geologist Notebook, take notes in the rain.* He saw her puzzled look. "In case you wonder, because I am a geologist as well as a private investigator, I prefer to take notes in these durable booklets. I learned to use them at the University of Arkansas. My undergraduate geology major required it. Now I'm partial to them. Rain can pour down, but my pencil writes on this special paper. Just so you know, I have two of these notebooks. One is for geological consulting and the other is for private investigations."

Sarah nodded. She gazed at the person in front of her. She had heard about Eric Bonfield from her geology professor, Gene McBride. In one of McBride's many sidebar stories, designed to keep his students from falling asleep, he had told of this unusual duck of a geologist who ran a private detective agency on the side. It wasn't until Danny's tragic death jarred her life that the story sparked Sarah's interest. Soon after her brother died from a fall off an oil rig on Sarah's farm, she had telephoned McBride. This morning's meeting with Eric Bonfield around Sarah's kitchen table was the result of that call.

Eric cleared his throat to get past her stare. "Ms. Isaacs, I'd like . . . ."

"Excuse me, Dr. Bonfield"—Sarah knew he had earned a doctorate in geology from the University of Illinois—"please call me *Sarah*. Everybody does."

"Certainly, Sarah, and I prefer *Eric*. I don't want people thinking I do medical work. As my father used to say, 'you're a doctor who doesn't do anybody any good!'"

Sarah laughed for the first time in many days. It felt good. A broad smile lightened her face. A warm glow returned to her cheeks after so many days of pale agony. She was ready to talk.

"Can we go back to what happened just before the death of your brother?" Eric asked.

Sarah nodded. "It started with these landmen who came to my house and offered to lease my farm property. They said there might be oil here. I'd never heard of anybody around this area finding oil, but I decided to give it a shot. I asked my attorney, who is my boss, to analyze the contract. I didn't want to be taken in by a scam. I've heard about those."

"That was a wise idea. What is the name of the company?"

"Arkwell Oil. I had never heard of them. Stan, the man I work for, said they operate in this part of Arkansas. The contract looked legit, so I signed it. I have a copy, if you'd like to see it."

"I'd eventually like to look it over, but please go ahead with your story."

"Well, it wasn't long until trucks rolled onto my property and began thumping the ground."

"Seismic vibrators," Eric interrupted. "Sound waves bounce off rock layers below ground and inform geologists about possible structures for oil accumulation."

"Yes. That's what they told me. It wasn't long after they left that I got another visit from a company rep who said they wanted to drill a test well. An oil rig appeared in days."

Eric frowned. "How long was it between rep visits and the oil rig?"

Sarah thought a moment. "The first reps came on a Saturday. I signed on the next Saturday. The trucks arrived on Wednesday and the oil rig a week from the following Saturday. Why do you ask? Is that a problem?"

"That is ridiculous! I never heard anyone ever make such a quick turnaround! You said they struck oil and are drilling other wells?"

"Yes." Sarah gave the time lines for those events.

Eric shook his head. "I'll need to see what formation they are after and do some technical work."

Sarah quickly cut in, "It's the Smackover Limestone. At least that's what the rep said."

Eric nodded approval. "The Smackover is a Jurassic age target for oil in Arkansas. Now all this activity of drilling and fracking was before the tragedy, right?"

"Yes." She paused and inhaled to avoid an outburst of tears.

Eric didn't press her. "This is hard for you, isn't it?"

Exhaling to clear her thoughts, she avoided answering his question. "I was fascinated by the whole operation. I watched everything from my house, using dad's field glasses. When they drilled the second well, I recognized a familiar figure high up on the rig. The way he moved and handled himself reminded me of Danny. I called his cell phone that evening and asked if it was him."

Sarah managed a weak smile. "He said, 'Yes', and told me what he did up there. He apologized for not calling me; as usual, he was too busy. That's just my brother . . . or was." Eric could see that she was on the verge of tears. Sarah took a deep breath and continued. "He called the place where he worked the *crow's nest* or *monkey board*. After he described his work, I told him it worried me because it looked so dangerous. He just laughed and said, 'Sis, you have nothing to be concerned about. I always follow protocol and wear a safety harness.' I had misgivings but tried to accept that he was safe up there."

"How long until he . . . er . . . fell?"

"Only two days after we talked on the phone. By then he had gone to a night shift."

"Did he say anything about his work after you first talked with him?"

Sarah paused. "I never heard from him again." The emotional tsunami rising within her welled over, and she began to cry.

Eric said nothing. He had grown up in a family of three boys and was uncomfortable when women cried. In high school he usually had waited until a girl could talk without crying before saying anything, but this technique didn't yield many dates. Girls considered him unresponsive.

Experience in the private detective business eventually helped Eric learn how to work with people under high stress. The turning point had come during a conversation with a woman who had hired him to investigate her husband's extramarital affairs. She told Eric, "I need you to listen to me. Make eye contact and say something to let me know you are listening!"

Remembering that learning experience, Eric sat quietly for a moment. Then he sighed before saying, "I have no idea how much pain this must be causing you."

She smiled weakly, blew into a tissue, and continued. "Thanks. The hurt is deep, but I must know what happened on that awful rig. The company's vagueness infuriates me."

"What did they tell you about Danny's fall?"

Sarah shook her head angrily. "What they didn't tell me is the problem!" Then she caught herself and lowered her voice. "I'll start with the phone call telling me they struck oil. I was so excited. The reps said another well would be drilled. That's when I first saw Danny in the crow's nest and later talked with him. The next time a rep called was to tell me that Danny had died on the rig. After Danny's funeral the company called again and said there had been no equipment failure. Danny simply fell to his death. That was all the rep said. End of story!" With wide eyes, Sarah looked imploringly at Eric, "What do you think?"

Staring down, Eric rose and began to pace back and forth. In a matter-of-fact voice, he said, "Most companies are reluctant to admit to any error on their part, so I'm not surprised at what the rep told you." He paused and cautiously proceeded, "Sarah, tell me about Danny. What was he like? Any hint of instability in his personality? Did he have friends? I'm after any clue."

Sarah tried to take control of her emotions. As she told Eric about her brother, she gestured vigorously. "Danny and I are very different people. I am older by three years and an organized person. I like to see things done well and proper. I am a planner. On the other hand, Danny is carefree . . . or he was." She paused and breathed deeply before continuing.

"He did things on the spur of the moment. It drove me nuts. Money ran through his fingers like water. That's one reason why Dad left him a trust account with a monthly allowance. No telling what Danny might do with a lot of cash. Danny's honesty wouldn't stand for anything illegal. He didn't do drugs or anything like that; he was just spontaneous.

"He had a strong faith. And he liked to help people, so a good sob story could quickly drain his wallet. Dad knew Danny's weakness and wanted to control his spending with the trust fund."

Sarah gave a deep sigh. "I guess I'm wandering, but I want you to know that Danny was as stable a person as you could meet. He had rock-solid faith in God and a happy disposition. His friends included a few hangers-on, but most were good, kind people. Danny took risks, but he avoided real danger. No one would ever say Danny was unstable."

Eric stopped pacing and listened to Sarah's glowing description of her brother. *Was Danny Isaacs really a saint?* Eric felt a growing need to talk with Danny's friends, as well as his co-workers on the oil rig. He asked, "Are there any clues that Danny might have been upset about something? Like at the oil rig?"

Sarah's face lit up. She went to a spare bedroom and emerged with a large box. "These are Danny's personal effects. Since I'm his closest relative, they came to me." She rummaged around in the box. "This looks like his cell phone, and here are a bunch of notes and papers. I've not taken time to go through them. Maybe something is in here. I'll see what I can find."

"Excellent, Sarah. I usually like to look through these sort of things, but you know your brother and might find a clue I could miss. As you go through all that, maybe you can discover something to help answer some questions. Call me when you discover anything at all."

Eric paused; then he spoke with professional formality: "I will take this investigation, Sarah. Something strange might have happened on the oil rig. Perhaps there may be reasons for how tight-lipped the oil company rep seems to be. There should be some documentation about safety meetings on this rig. These organizations try to protect their interests. Any blame that can be shifted away from themselves is to their benefit. Maybe I can find what's below the surface."

Sarah breathed a huge sigh. "Thank you, Eric."

"A lot is left unmentioned in what the company told you. I'll need to visit their offices. But I want to hit the well site first. If I can get interviews with the roughnecks on the tower or from the tool pusher, something might turn up. While I'm doing that maybe you'll find a clue in this box. I want to know what was going on right before Danny's death. And I'll need a list of associates from his cell phone."

"Of course," said Sarah. "Thank you for listening to me ramble on and for taking the investigation. I really want to know what happened to Danny."

As Eric walked to the front door, Sarah followed and took his hand. She squeezed it and smiled into those beautiful blue eyes. He smiled back. Her warm hand gave him a pleasant sensation. They parted wordlessly. Eric drove to the rig and turned his attention to the roughnecks.

Sarah watched as Eric drove toward the pasture where an oil rig chugged noisily in the late evening shadows. She turned back to the kitchen that held so many family memories. She took a deep breath. Then she emptied Danny's box onto the kitchen table. With her laptop on a side table and opened to a spreadsheet, Sarah was ready to organize the jumble of items.

Chapter 2

As Sarah began an inventory of Danny's belongings, her mind drifted to family. None were living. Sadness overwhelmed her for a few minutes. But slowly, pleasant memories pushed darkness aside. Remembering her mother, Sarah smiled . . .

* * * * * *

When Mom was diagnosed with cancer during Sarah's high school years, the news struck fear in the family. But her mother refused to give in to the disease. She maintained a composure that a strong believer in God can have in such situations. Her body refused to respond to treatments, and she died before Sarah graduated from high school. Mom's legacy of love stayed with Sarah.

She remembered once, during her sophomore year, crying on Mom's shoulder about the way the football cheerleaders looked down at the cheerleaders for women's basketball. "They think they are so good," Sarah complained. "They make me feel like dirt." Those were the girls who jumped and tumbled to the delight of ogling high school boys. Sarah wanted no part of those exhibitions. Adding to her basketball cheerleading companions' misery, lots of people attended the football games, but only a few die-hard students and parents showed up for women's basketball games. It felt odd to cheer with hardly anyone in the stands.

Sarah remembered her mother had said, "Sarah, those basketball girls need you to cheer for them. The football cheering squad is just showing off." Sarah needed no more encouragement. After that conversation, she worked hard to build enthusiasm for women's basketball.

Mom's wisdom also helped when the football girls made the homecoming court, and her squad didn't even have a runner-up. "Who cares?" became Sarah's response to the social segregation that dominated high school girls. As a first born, she had developed a self-possession which carried her past squirrely, giggly girls who became pregnant before high school ended. She remembered her Dad saying that he was proud to be the father of a woman with a wise head on her shoulders. She blushed when he said this, but inwardly she was thankful for his support.

* * * * * *

Sarah returned to the task of logging Danny's belongings and searching for clues.

Eric arrived at the active oil rig and asked if he could speak with men who were on site when Danny died. "No problem," said the tool pusher. "Some who were on that shift are on break now."

Eric approached a well-built man sipping water. Joseph Hernandez spoke English with only a trace of his heritage from Mexico. After introductions, Eric asked, "Joseph, what do you remember about the fall of Danny Isaacs?"

"I remember quite a bit. I was on his shift that night. The whole thing was very strange," Joseph began. "Danny was not his usual happy self when he came to work. I didn't have time to ask why, because our tower was short-handed, and Danny needed to get up to his monkey board in a hurry."

"Did you see Danny fall?"

"Not exactly. I turned around when I heard him scream . . . ."

"What! Danny screamed? What did he say?"

10

"It was an awful scream." Joseph paused, looked around, and hesitantly said, "It was maybe like . . . I don't know . . . maybe . . . 'Nooo'."

"Anything besides, 'Nooo'?"

"It is hard to say. Equipment is loud . . . and I was not close to him as he fell."

"How far away were you when he fell?" Eric asked.

"I was working far from the rig. That is why I could hear him scream. Those nearby could not hear because of the noise on the rig."

Something about Joseph's description sounded less than genuine to Eric. *I think you know more but are holding something back.* "Did you examine Danny after the fall?"

"Yes, I ran to Danny, but there was no life in him."

"Any visible marks on his body?"

Joseph shrugged. "I don't think so. I was shaken and didn't check him very well."

"Was Danny wearing the safety harness when you found him?"

"No. And when I looked around there were not any parts of the harness on the ground. That puzzled me."

"Were there other witnesses to the fall?"

"Yes, I saw three other guys run over to check on Danny." He gave Eric their names.

"Joseph, thank you. You have been a great help. If you think of anything else, would you let me know? Here's my card."

The next two roughnecks added nothing to Joseph's account. The third worker, Jon, a ruddy young man with bright red hair, gave Eric one additional bit of information. "Before I worked the rigs, I was an EMT for an Arkansas ambulance service company," Jon said. "By habit, I took the time to examine Danny. I found something really strange."

"What's that?" Eric's mind snapped to attention.

"I found a scrape-burn on the side of his face."

"What might have caused the burn?"

"Well, I've worked the monkey board myself. Of course, I used the harness. The burn on the side of Danny's face matched the width of the harness straps. I guess the straps could have rubbed against Danny's face as he started to fall from the railed platform."

"Tell me what that might look like."

Jon said the only scenario he could imagine involved Danny falling out of the harness, and the straps rubbing against him as he fell.

"How could straps do that?" Eric asked.

"The only thing I can think of is either the back straps of the harness were cut or they failed. Danny's weight would have forced the front straps of the harness to rub against him as he fell."

"The harness might have been cut?" Eric exclaimed. "That suggests foul play! Do you know if investigators examined the harness?"

"Can't say. We aren't allowed to hang around during investigations."

Eric kept probing but Jon added nothing more that seemed to relate directly to the fall.

"Can I call you if I think of something?" Jon asked.

"You bet," said Eric. He gave Jon his card and thanked him.

Walking away, Eric thought about what Jon said. *Jon's analysis doesn't jibe with the official report that there was "no equipment failure." I need to interview the company investigator.*

The tool pusher provided phone numbers and addresses of company offices. Eric almost ran to his pickup.

Phone calls to Arkwell Oil's safety office yielded only monotonous voice mail greetings. *No night investigators.*

The next-best source of information should be the police in Little Rock, so Eric drove to Precinct #2 station, which shared jurisdiction of Sarah's farm with the sheriff. The officer in charge of the accident investigation unit was on night duty. His brief statement labeled the fall as an accident or possible suicide.

"Why do you say that?" Eric asked skeptically.

The officer shrugged his shoulders. "Not much to go on. Guy falls from a high place. He's the only one up there. Looks like carelessness or suicide, wouldn't you think?"

"Not necessarily," said Eric. "Did you inspect the safety harness?"

"No, the company investigator said there was no equipment failure, so we let it go at that."

Eric bristled. "You didn't bother to check the harness?"

"Hey, we trust these guys," the officer said. "We've worked with them before. No problem."

"Could you give me the name of the company investigator?"

"Sure, it's Spencer Frye. Nice guy."

"Thanks," said Eric, but without enthusiasm. *Talk about a run-around.*

Chapter 3

*E*ric went to Sarah's home after she returned from work the next day and told her what he had learned so far. "I want to put my hands on that harness. Did Danny ever talk about the harness?"

"Not much, except to assure me that it was perfectly safe."

"Well," Eric said, "I did some quick checking online about falls from crow's nests. Causes are mostly due to not wearing a harness or faulty harnesses. No examples of suicide. Danny's death could be a mistake on his part or a flawed harness. The only other alternative, according to police, and presumably the company investigators, is suicide."

"It can't be suicide," Sarah insisted, the fire in her eyes speaking volumes. "Not Danny. He was a well-balanced person who loved life."

Changing the subject, Eric said, "Did you find anything in the box of Danny's things that hinted of a problem?"

Sarah pulled out a scrap of paper. "There is this," handing him the note.

He read the paper aloud. "Something is going on. This bothers me." Eric looked at Sarah. "Do you have any idea what was bothering him?"

Sarah shook her head. "No. That's the only hint of any problem I can find in all these papers. Danny loved his job. I don't know if the note refers to work or something else. There is no date on the paper."

Eric read the paper again. "I'll keep this in the back of my mind as I talk with his friends. Maybe they know something. Do you have a list from Danny's cell phone?"

"Yes," Sarah said, handing him a neatly printed sheet. "Danny never deleted any text messages. I've sorted through the names and phone numbers."

"Great. That is a big help. I'll check with some of his friends and also try to find that harness, if it still exists." He paused. "I assume there were no clues about this concern of Danny's in the text messages?"

"None whatsoever," Sarah said emphatically. "Either he decided it wasn't important enough to share, or this note was written very recently and he hadn't been able to talk about it with anyone."

"Danny's note could be another piece of the puzzle that may or may not be important in solving why he fell," said Eric. His forehead was furrowed as he tried to process what little information there was to go on.

Sarah thanked Eric for what he had discovered and gave him a hug as he left. He smiled and promised to keep her up to date.

As he drove away, Eric wondered about Sarah's hug. Then he shrugged it off. *She's probably from a family of huggers.* He headed to a small café for a very late supper before collapsing for the night.

Sarah stood in her doorway as Eric drove away. *His dark brown hair matches mine. Nice bod too.* She laughed at herself and turned back to her kitchen. *Maybe all my fussing about Danny's death will lead to an answer about why he died. Maybe Eric Bonfield can find that answer."* She smiled as she thought again of his hair color.

Sarah wasn't ready for bed. She hadn't cleaned the house since Danny died, so she decided to clean it—tonight. *Time to do a job worthy of the parents who left me this farm.* Inspired, she grabbed supplies and vacuum and set to work. Cleaning the house triggered memories, and Sarah began thinking about her father . . .

* * * * * *

In some ways, her dad's death was more tragic than her mother's. Mom's prolonged illness allowed the family to grieve over a period of years.

But Dad's death was sudden. He always plowed the east field every fall. He knew to avoid one of the many gullies that etched that part of their farm, but heavy rain had fallen the week before and the easternmost gully had become a muddy bank that loomed before him sooner than he expected. His tractor and plow slid into the ravine, throwing him from his seat, and pinning him under a plow blade.

The phone call came to Sarah just as she was leaving Stan's office. "Your father . . . critical condition . . . St. Joseph's hospital . . . come fast." Terrified, she jumped into her car and sped to the ER. Her mind raced. Years earlier she had lost her mother to cancer, and now . . . her father . . . . *I mustn't think those thoughts.* She pushed harder on the accelerator.

The emergency room physician met Sarah outside her father's room with the sad news that he had died while she was in route. Sarah felt her legs give way as she staggered into the room where her loving and supportive father lay lifeless from a crushed chest and broken arms.

Sarah collapsed in a heap of tears by her father's bedside. Denial rushed in. *How could this happen? He was such a careful farmer. He was a good man. He lived a life of faith. He was young. Why would God take him so soon?* No answers came. Sarah felt numb. Finally, she struggled to rise from the bedside, and a nurse led her to the front door of the hospital.

Danny had been working at a job west of Little Rock when Sarah phoned him. He raced into the hospital parking lot just as Sarah was fumbling with her car keys. "What happened to Dad?" Fear choked his voice.

Sarah managed a tearful, gasping response. "He . . . he's gone!" Her words were barely understandable. Speech seemed to stick to her tongue.

"No, it can't be!" Danny's high-pitched voice bounced off the hospital's white brick walls.

Sarah tried to explain, but her words were garbled. All the sister and brother could do was hold one another tightly, crying until they ran out of tears. Then Danny helped Sarah into her car. He gently closed her door. He could barely speak. "Can ... can you drive?" Sarah nodded weakly. She started the engine and drove out of the hospital lot. Sick with uncertainty, Danny stared after her. When her taillights disappeared around a corner, he turned to walk toward the emergency room door. He dreaded what he would see.

Somehow Sarah made it to her apartment without knowing how she got there. She turned off the engine and sat in her car for several minutes without any idea what to do next. Normally she would be hungry after eight hours at the law office, but she had no interest in food. Her father's death weighed so heavily on her heart that her mind seemed far away. She climbed the steps to her apartment door. Her confusion made finding the right key a chore. Once inside, Sarah slumped into a living room chair. At last, she decided she should at least try to sleep. There would be much to do in the days ahead. Her orderly mind was starting to push through the suffocating emotion.

Her father's funeral befitted a man who faithfully attended church, gave generously, and encouraged his family to love God. The service moved slowly—she was too numb to take in what Pastor Daniels said. Her mind tried to grasp what was happening. *I feel like an outside observer looking through a window.* Then she felt Danny's strong arm around her shoulders. He said nothing, but his touch meant everything. *My brother's love will carry me through this.* She relaxed slightly.

After the service, friends spoke kind words and praised her father. *They mean well, but my head is spinning . . . my world is upside-down.* Everything felt surreal.

The next few days blurred as Sarah's grief deepened. Her parents were both dead. Sarah felt alone. Only her brother remained. After the burial, Danny had returned to work. He promised to call; she would need to hear his voice during the coming days.

One morning, after the funeral, Sarah's phone rang. It was Stan, her attorney and boss. He asked if she felt like coming to his office. "Not to work, but to go over your father's will. When can you and Danny come in?"

A few days later she and Danny met Stan for the reading of the will. Stan read aloud the carefully prepared trust their father wisely had drawn up years earlier. Sarah received the farm. It was paid for. Danny would receive regular payments from a fund set up for him.

Sarah sat amazed at her father's wisdom. *Dad's arrangements make a lot of sense.* She, the business-minded of the two siblings, could rent the land to local farmers, using her college courses to provide business models. Danny, on the other hand, was anything but business-oriented. He didn't handle money well, so small draws from the trust fund should work well for him.

Danny told Sarah he liked the arrangement. He preferred money to farm work. "Dad was smart. This setup matches my lifestyle. Enjoy the farm, Sis." Sarah smiled slightly as she kissed Danny on the cheek. They parted with a hug. Danny phoned Sarah once a week for a couple months. Then his calls became less frequent. Sarah understood that Danny's free spirit kept him from communicating with her on a regular basis. *It's just the way he's wired.*

Since the trust avoided probate, Sarah could immediately do with the farm as she wished. It didn't take her long to decide to move back home. Little Rock held nothing for her except a job. No steady boyfriend occupied her time, and her few girlfriends could be reached with a short drive. Moving back to the farmhouse where she had grown up suited her well. It gave her a sense of closeness to her parents, and it wasn't a long drive to work.

Sarah moved from her apartment at the end of the month. The well-maintained farm house needed few changes to become home again. Soon her life developed a new pattern: her work in Little Rock helped her escape boredom and sadness while she applied her business training to running the farm. Things settled into a routine, but routines are made to be broken. That's when Arkwell Oil entered her life.

* * * * * *

Sarah finished cleaning the last room in the house, looked at her work approvingly, and put the equipment and supplies away. If she hadn't been tired earlier, she was worn out now. During what remained of the night, she slept soundly for the first time in days. Good thing. She would need it.

Chapter 4

*D*awn brought the morning bright and clear. Eric yawned and stretched. The number of things he needed to do exceeded the hours in a day. Finding the suspicious harness could offer a key piece of evidence, but interviewing people might be more important right now. Memories can evaporate as time passes. Eric decided to speak with Danny's friends first. If a key person moved away, that might be a problem.

Finding the names on the list Sarah gave him was not easy. Danny ran around with a small crowd of young men who liked what he liked and did things together just for fun. They weren't into drugs, alcohol, or crime, as far as Sarah knew. They just loved action! Eric finally corralled Merlin Franklin, one of Danny's close friends, and they sat down to talk.

"I got no clue why Danny died," Merlin declared. "Danny loved life as much as anybody. We had a lot of laughs and did plenty of fun stuff." Merlin paused and breathed a deep sigh. "I just can't imagine that Danny would take his life by jumping' off an oil rig. No Way! Besides, Danny was very religious. I never heard him make self-threats, and he never seemed depressed."

"How about enemies? Any people Danny didn't get along with?"

"Not that I know of. He never talked much about anyone in particular."

"What do you mean, 'in particular'? Details are important."

"Oh, some jerk thought Danny was messing around with his girl."

"Really? Tell me about it."

"There was this guy—Bodien Kessel—he hassled Danny about Jean."

"Who is Jean?"

"Oh, she's somebody Danny dated a couple times. He met her through a friend, I guess, and they went out a little. It never amounted to much. She seemed kind of different." Eric took notes as Merlin talked.

"I don't know much about Bodien Kessel," Merlin added. "I just know he considered Jean his private property, and he was really mad at Danny for seeing her."

"Do you know where Kessel lives?" Eric wrote down the general location. Then he asked, "When did Danny talk about Kessel?"

"Come to think of it, not long before he died."

Eric thought of one more question: "Do you know Jean's address?" Merlin thought Kessel and Jean lived close to each other, but he didn't know their addresses.

Eric thought a moment. "Look, Merlin, if you think of anything else, give me a call at this number, OK?"

"Sure thing, Eric. I hope you find what caused Danny's fall."

"Oh, I think we will."

In his pickup, Eric reviewed his conversation with Merlin. He now had two more names—Bodien Kessel and Jean—to add to his list of persons to interview. *Jean . . . what's her last name?* Eric shook his head. *I must be slipping.* He dialed Merlin's number. "Hey Merlin, I need Jean's last name."

"Glad you called," Merlin answered. "I did a little checking myself and found something you might be interested in. Bodien Kessel was found last night shot to death!"

"What! How did it happen?"

"Well, they found him, of all places, on Sarah Isaacs' farm not far from an oil rig."

"Any details?" asked Eric, wide-eyed.

"Not that I know of. The police blotter is pretty sketchy."

"Thanks, Merlin, you've been a big help. Oh, by the way, do you know Jean's last name?"

"Yes, it's Myers."

Eric stared into space for a minute as he tried to put this new wrinkle onto the face of Danny's death. Ideas, motives, and random thoughts burst into his mind. *Were these two deaths related? They almost had to be since both men died on Sarah's farm. I wonder if Sarah knew anything about Kessel. Why was he on her farm last night? I want to find that harness, but everything must wait. I'd better get to Sarah's place right away.*

He found Sarah sitting on her front porch. It was an attractive farm house that was above the average Arkansas farmstead. The red brick with white wood siding was well-maintained. This was a tribute to Sarah's father. The siding looked as though it had never lacked a fresh coat of paint. The porch was decorated with colorful flower pots. A swing and rocking chair invited lazy afternoon conversations. Sarah was gently moving back and forth in the swing. She hardly seemed to see anything that wasn't directly in front of her, and she didn't notice when Eric parked in the driveway. Eric cautiously approached the porch and called out softly, "Sarah?"

Startled, she said, "Oh, I'm sorry, Eric. I've been so spaced since I heard about Bodien's murder . . . on my property."

"Did you know him?"

Sarah hesitated. Her answer seemed guarded, "Only slightly. He ran with a crowd I didn't approve of. My only contact with him was through Jean Myers."

"So you know Jean Myers?"

"Yes, we were in high school together. We were cheerleaders for the women's basketball team. After graduation, we went to a local college, but she dropped out and started working."

"Have you seen her lately?"

Sarah paused before answering. "Not much. I am so confused. Bodien is dead. Killed on my farm! Why?"

"That's a big question. Any ideas? Did he ever show up here before?"

Another pause. "Yes, he came with Jean once. Just a social visit. Said he wanted to see the oil rig in action. Of course, he couldn't get very close without supervision. They hung around a little while and left."

"Sarah, do you know if Danny ever dated Jean?"

She looked up quickly with a wary face. "Where did you hear that?"

"One of Danny's friends said they went out a couple times. That got Bodien upset; he was mad at Danny."

Sarah's response seemed cautious. "Danny wouldn't have dated Jean," she declared. "Jean was not his type!"

"What do you mean by that?"

"Oh, Jean's been in trouble with the law off and on; she's done drugs and shoplifting. She'd be more of a project for Danny than someone to date. Danny never dated girls much, that is . . . ." Sarah's voice trailed off; her eyes mirrored her frustration.

"Maybe that was it," said Eric. "Maybe he wanted to help her."

Sarah changed the subject. "Bodien was a terrible influence on Jean and the worst person in her life."

"Do you know where she lives?"

"Yes. I'll give you her address."

"Are you well enough for me to leave and check out some things?"

Sarah responded bitterly, "Don't worry about me. I've only lost all my family and now have a murder, or two, on my property."

A worried look passed over Eric's face. Cautiously he said, "I have a friend who could come and stay with you for a while. She might give you some company. It's awfully quiet out here, except for the oil rig."

Sarah turned to him and her opinion of Eric as a caring person jumped to a new level. *He is more than just a private eye with a PhD.* Reaching up, she kissed him on the cheek. "Thank you, Eric. It would be very nice to have someone around."

Eric looked startled. "Um, I'll ask someone from my church to come." And he hurried away.

Back in his pickup, Eric called Julie McPherson. She said, "I'm glad to help a friend!"

Then he gathered his thoughts and planned his next interview. He wanted to talk with Jean Myers. She might provide some missing pieces to the strange collage of events at Sarah's farm. At first it had seemed like a fairly simple case: Danny's death—a man falls from an oil rig. It's not common, but it happens. Is it an accident, suicide, or murder? Those were the possibilities Eric came up with. *But how can the death of Bodien near the oil rig be related to Danny's fall?*

His four years in the oil business as a site geologist had exposed Eric to accidents on rigs. He didn't recall ever witnessing someone who fell from the monkey board, but he had read about it. The guys on record who did fall? Well, he read that some were too cocky, too cool, too sloppy, or whatever. Macho types might ignore the harness once—they had never needed it before. They liked the freedom of movement. Then it would happen. A section of drill pipe would swing out too far. They would reach for it and slip over the edge never to be cocky again. Surviving a fall of many tens of feet onto a hard platform is unlikely.

The burn on Danny's face didn't necessarily fit an accident scenario. Burns can come from hot pipes, cables, or fluids. *Had there been foul play? What I need is that harness. If it's been tampered with or shows faulty construction, then Danny's death was not a suicide. Somebody would be responsible.*

But where did Bodien fit in? And what about Danny's cryptic note of concern? Torn between finding the harness and Jean's involvement, Eric decided to visit Jean. He drove to her address which was in a depressed part of Little Rock. Boarded-up buildings, trash-filled streets, and people shuffling aimlessly down cracked sidewalks did not speak well of the area. The outside of Jean's apartment house needed either a paint job or the building needed a wrecking ball. The entry door barely hung on its hinges. Eric tapped a loose button dangling from an exposed wire, and a rude voice called, "Who's there?"

Eric identified himself and Jean buzzed him in. He knocked on Apartment Number 8, and a tall woman cautiously opened the door. "I . . . I . . . don't want to talk," she stammered.

Eric tried to calm her. "Look, I'm a private investigator working for Sarah Isaacs on the death of her brother. I don't want to cause you any pain, but I'd like to ask a few questions."

Mentioning Sarah's name helped. Hesitantly, Jean let him in and led him to a worn couch in what probably was the living room. Jean sat on a folding chair with uneven legs. She was taller than Sarah, and her lightened hair needed a redo. Her makeup was smeared; her clothes were wrinkled. Her shifting brown eyes screamed a distrust of anyone in authority.

Fumbling with a cigarette, Jean said, "The police been here all morning."

Eric spoke calmly, "Jean, would you talk about your last visit to Sarah's farm, the one with Bodien Kessel?"

Jean eyed Eric with uncertainty. She hesitated before she said slowly, "That wasn't the last time I seen Sarah at her farm."

Eric's eyes blinked; Sarah had said Jean was only an infrequent visitor. "Well, tell me whatever you'd like to say about your visits to Sarah's place."

Warming up to Eric slightly, Jean began a long discourse about how she and Sarah had been cheerleaders for the high school girls' basketball team. Jean paused nervously as she spoke. After high school, Sarah talked her into attending college with her, but she didn't take well to the studies and dropped out. She considers Sarah her only real friend and respects her. After her failed college experience, Jean took a job as bar maid in a local dive. That was where she met Bodien Kessel. He was the only guy who paid attention to her. Bodien was always hanging around, even when she changed jobs, which she did frequently.

Jean often visited the farm after the death of Sarah's father. "Sarah told me to ditch my other friends. Then she introduced me to Danny. He told me the same thing. He said to get rid of my chums. He wanted me to do somethin' with my life. We dated a few times but nothin' romantic happened." Jean's face saddened.

"Danny told me to move out of this dump and stop seein' Bodien. This ticked off Bodien and I warned Danny to stay clear of him. So did Sarah." Eric listened and nodded. Jean's story didn't exactly match Sarah's version.

"Those folks tried to help me. I listened to them. I even went to church once! How about that?

"Then one day Bodien wanted to look at the oil thing on Sarah's farm. But Sarah didn't want Bodien on her property. So we left. I been back a little by myself."

Why did Sarah keep some of this from me? Eric needed the whole story to find any connection between the two deaths. He pushed the big question into their conversation: "Jean, do you know why Bodien died on Sarah's farm?" Jean looked down and hesitated. She knew something.

"I . . . he . . . well, it was about Danny's death. That's all I know for sure." She spoke too fast; too loud.

"What do you think was the connection?"

Jean fumbled with her cigarette. "He said he had somethin' to do. I got no idea what it was." Jean's clumsy answer clearly avoided what she knew.

"Do you think Bodien had anything to do with Danny's fall?" Eric asked.

Jean turned defensive and stammered, "I . . . don't know."

"Why did Bodien go to the farm?"

Jean's frustration peaked. She stood up. "I don't know nothin'."

This conversation is over. "Well, thanks, Jean. If you think of more details about Bodien, Danny, or Sarah, let me know. Here's my card."

Jean quickly showed Eric out. As the door closed, Eric heard the lock turn, followed by a huge sigh.

Now that was interesting. I need to square her story with Sarah's. Somebody is spinning a tale or has something to hide.

Chapter 5

*W*hile Sarah waited nervously for Eric's friend to arrive and provide company, she mulled over the events that had led to Arkwell Oil's invasion of the family farm . . .

* * * * * *

Farm life had never appealed to Sarah when she was younger. She loved academics more than vegetable gardens or cows. Although she was attractive, Sarah had not dated much in high school—few guys wanted to date an "egghead". The summer after her graduation from high school she enrolled in the local community college, finishing with an Associate Degree in Business two years later.

About that time, a small law office in Little Rock had advertised for a secretary. Sarah was offered the position, and her father encouraged her to take the job. She moved to Little Rock and rented a small apartment near the law office. The responsibilities of a legal secretary appealed to her sense of order, and soon she settled into a routine. Stan, her boss and the only attorney at the office, recognized her hard work and rewarded her generously with increases in salary. She accumulated a small savings account, which she planned to use when she bought a house.

Then came her father's tragic death. Sarah moved back to the farm, glad to reconnect with this remnant of her past. Commuting to Little Rock wasn't a problem, as the farm was an easy drive to the city. Sarah was glad to be back home. Country life proved to be a pleasing contrast to her work in town; at the farm she could relax. Other farmers rented the land for row crops and cattle.

One Saturday morning, a white sedan pulled up in front of her farm house. Two men in business suits identified themselves as representatives of Arkwell Oil. They announced that they had a proposal: her farm might be sitting on an oil field, and Arkwell Oil would like to lease the farmland with an option to drill. Sarah was astounded. The men gave her a copy of a hefty proposal for her to sign. Sarah told them she would give the proposal consideration; she wanted to talk with her attorney first.

After the Arkwell reps left, Sarah brewed a cup of tea and sat at the kitchen table to think. She remembered a geology course she had taken as an elective at the community college. She knew that independent oil companies specialized in small wildcat operations that bigger companies tended to pass over. Maybe Arkwell Oil was one such company.

Sarah called Stan, and he agreed to read the contract Monday morning. Hanging up the phone, she said aloud, "Whatever Stan says I will do. I'm way out of my league."

Sarah didn't sleep much that night. In church the next morning she could hardly keep focused on the sermon. Visions of oil rigs kept dancing in her imagination. That afternoon she did a computer search on wildcat wells. Sarah knew that a wildcat well was drilled in an area not yet developed or known for extracting petroleum. She could hardly wait for Stan to read the contract and give his assessment of it.

Monday morning finally came. Sarah drove to work as fast as she dared push her little car. She parked and raced into the office. Stan was reading the *Wall Street Journal*. He put down his coffee cup and laid the newspaper aside. Stan was familiar with the legal aspects of drilling for oil and oil companies. As he carefully studied the document, he made a few notes.

"Sarah, I don't see anything out of the ordinary here," Stan said, looking up. "Reimbursement is ample, and I see no problems. It doesn't look like a scam."

"What do you think I should do?" Sarah asked. "Are there any limitations on how I use my property? How could Arkwell use it?"

Stan explained how an oil company's lease works. "Based on some tests, they may or may not actually drill for oil or natural gas." Stan paused to choose the correct words. "My recommendation is that it might be in your best interest to sign the contract. Perhaps nothing will come of it, or perhaps you'll get lucky. Either way, you can still farm the land."

The following Saturday, when the two Arkwell reps returned, Sarah signed the contract. The men told her that geophysical surveyors would begin their work in a few days. Sarah was thrilled. She spent much of the afternoon looking on the internet for more information about oil wells, oil prospecting, and drilling. Sarah wanted to learn as much as she could. She read the articles ravenously.

* * * * * *

The arrival of Eric's friend to sit with Sarah cut her memory visit short. Julie, a perky blond of about thirty, bounced through the door and gave Sarah a hug. "I hear you might like some company. Well, I'm it!" Sarah smiled and led Julie to the well-used kitchen table where they munched on cookies and drank coffee while Julie told about her latest vacation to the Rocky Mountains.

Chapter 6

*I*t was mid-afternoon, and Eric had not yet contacted Arkwell management or interviewed Danny's other friends or located the harness. A day just wasn't long enough!

His cell phone buzzed. "Hi Megan. What's up?" Eric's office manager ran the business side of operations. She had three grown children and a husband with a great job, so she didn't need to work, but she had time on her hands and wanted something challenging to do. When she answered Eric's help-wanted ad, he recognized that she had the qualities he needed in his office. She started the next day after the interview. The diversity of Eric's work fit her personality, and she soon had the office running smoothly.

"Eric, you've got lots of e-mails and phone calls to answer; work is piling up," Megan said briskly. "When are you coming to the office?"

"Oops. Sorry Megan! I've been so busy with this oil field incident that I let other things slip. What's urgent?"

"Well, your report on Sam Erickson's drainage problem is due tomorrow. The Jenson's radon recommendation could stand some attention. And, of course, Mrs. Radley calls every afternoon to be reassured that her derelict husband stays behind bars. Need some more?"

Eric groaned. "I've got to write that report so Sam's field isn't flooded by the next monsoon. I'll come in later and do that. Maybe I can look at the data on radon levels too."

"I'll talk to Mrs. Radley myself," Megan offered.

"Thanks. You're a gem. Don't know what I ever did without you."

"Don't get gushy, Eric; you just need somebody to keep you organized."

"You're right about that! See ya!"

So the rest of his day was predestined. He'd postpone seeing Sarah until tomorrow. Julie should provide enough company for Sarah until he could visit again. *Maybe I can check with the Arkwell accident investigator this afternoon— better yet, I could stop there on my way to the office.* Since he had been unable to make contact directly by phone, a spontaneous visit might be the best way to find the person.

The investigator's office occupied a tiny shop with a drooping sign in a worn-out strip mall. *What a dump!* The door rattled when he knocked. Somebody inside loudly responded, "Come on in, the water's fine!" Eric pushed the creaking door open until it bumped against a table leg. "What can I do you for?" asked a jovial man who, from his waist size, might live off doughnuts and ice cream.

"Hello. I'm Eric Bonfield, a private investigator working on an oil field incident: the fall of one Danny Isaacs. I'm looking for whoever investigated the incident."

The man's countenance switched almost instantly to a defiant glare. "Private Detective, eh? Well, I'm Spencer Frye, and I can tell you the guy fell and died as a result. What else do you want to know?"

"Do you have a report on your findings?"

"Yeah, but I need to see some I.D. and a release signed by Ms. Isaacs."

Eric had anticipated this request, and he produced the signed release. He showed this to Frye, who fumbled with a folder and handed Eric a one-page document. Eric glanced at the brief statement and then looked up at Frye. "This document states only that Danny Isaacs fell from a high level platform on a rig and died. Is that all? Aren't there testimonies of witnesses or descriptions of the scene; any ideas about how it happened?"

"Nope," Frye said. "Our job is just to report facts. Obviously nobody pushed the man. Must have slipped. Probably didn't wear a harness. That's about it."

"Did anyone inspect the harness?"

"No, why should we? It wasn't attached to him when we inspected the situation. As far as I know the harness is still in use on the rig that's drilling right now."

Appalled, Eric stared at Arkwell's accident investigator. He had never seen such sloppy investigative work. He asked, "Did the Little Rock police investigate? Did any State police come out?"

"Yeah. A city cop showed up, took a few pictures, grabbed our notes and left. State people are too busy with other accidents. They copied my statement and the police report."

There was obviously no need to continue the conversation. *This guy is either lying or totally incompetent!* "Thanks for the information," Eric said with little sincerity. "Do you know the name of the officer with the photos?"

"Wilson, Second Precinct."

Eric left the Arkwell office, biting his lip to avoid telling Frye what he thought of their "investigation."

The police station lay on Eric's route to his office, so he stopped there and asked for Wilson. The officer was serving desk duty. He made copies of the photos for Eric, but there was nothing new in them, except one photo that clearly showed the burn mark on Danny's face.

"What did you make of this mark on the man's face?" asked Eric.

Wilson shrugged. "Probably got it when he fell." That was obvious, but Eric decided not to pursue the discussion. Grudgingly, he thanked Officer Wilson and took copies of the photos with him.

As he drove to his office, Eric tried to move past his emotional reactions to what seemed to be a lack of competence on the part of Arkwell's accident investigator and the inefficiency of the police. *What is going on? Do these people know nothing about how to investigate a death? Is there a cover-up? Are the oil company and the local law colluding? Why such a skimpy report about a violent death? If I am supposed to help Sarah know the cause of her brother's death, I'll need lots more evidence.*

Arriving at the neighborhood of low-slung buildings where his office sat, Eric's thoughts shifted from anger to analysis. His scientific background resurfaced, and he began to think of data he would need to probe through the confusion of today. Somewhere in the maze of events surrounding Sarah Isaac's farm, there had to be answers to questions about the cause of Danny Isaac's death.

Eric maintained an office that included a small lab room for simple analysis of geological samples gathered for his consulting business. He did basic lab work himself but farmed out more sophisticated analytical studies to professional labs. On the private detective side of his business, Eric required access to large databases kept by law enforcement agencies and other government sources. One of Megan's many skills involved the gathering and organization of both geological and criminal data. Eric relied on her to dig deep into databases while he did leg work.

Megan's habit was to put things in order before she left for the day. When Eric arrived long after closing time, he found phone messages, papers, and reports neatly stacked on his desk. There were also extensive computer files that awaited his attention. He absently looked through the pile, gave a sigh, and settled into his desk chair. Its squeak irritated him; if only he could remember to ask Megan to order a replacement. For some reason, he didn't think of leaving her a note or an e-mail. The Danny Isaacs case clouded his mind.

The pile of work involved an assortment of geological and private detective problems. Eric enjoyed geological consulting. It gave him contact with real people who needed a geologist's expertise to help them with environmental issues. His clients included many local residents with problems such as drainage, flooding, or sinkhole collapse. Large companies also called on him from time to time for short-term projects.

On the other side of his ledger, Eric became known by local law enforcement officials because of his success in finding criminals and his ability to gather evidence needed to send them to prison. His abilities drew admiration in wider and wider circles. Someday, being known might open doors otherwise difficult to enter.

Eric's eyes fell on a phone message from Cindy Merkie. Cindy owned a quarter section of land next to a famous Arkansas quartz mine. This caught his attention long enough to read her request. Cindy's little rock shop sold quartz crystals. Her third-rate stand struggled next to a big store which attracted tourists from outside Arkansas. Recently a new quartz vein on Cindy's property revealed high-quality crystals. Would Eric come out and take a look?

The request intrigued Eric, so he made a note for Megan to call Cindy about an appointment. Many of the items on Eric's desk could wait, so he turned to the most urgent projects. Three hours later, Eric piled reports and messages on Megan's desk or sent them as attachments to her e-mail. He yawned and stretched. His chair squeaked.

Although a geologist with a reasonable consulting business, Eric loved private detective work. Private investigation consumed well over half his time. It paid better than the low-end of geological consulting, but it wasn't the money that attracted him. Private investigation work made him feel worthwhile but so did the geology side of his business. He was picky about cases he accepted. If he didn't find something challenging or helpful for people, he turned down jobs, even when they promised significant cash.

Eric found meaning in finding solutions that satisfied his clients and himself. That was one reason he had chosen consulting over working for a big multi-national. How else could he be both a geologist and a private investigator? Why did he like both of these areas? It all boiled down to solving problems. His background in geologic training served him well in the two fields.

To Eric, solving crimes and doing geology were very much alike. He used the same thought patterns whether he was working through geological problems or investigating criminal activity. He gathered facts and generated possible solutions to explain what had happened. In both areas he developed ideas to make sense of data. Geological private detective or private detective-geologist, it didn't matter. Either title described him well.

By now the wall clock read 10:30 p.m. and Eric felt bushed. He got up to turn out the light when his cell phone jingled. *Why would someone call so late?*

"Eric, this is Sarah. Can you come over right away?"

"Uh, well, yes, I guess I can. It will take me a while to get there."

What can she want at this hour? He turned off the light, locked the door to his office, and headed for his pickup. Muggy air greeted him in the still smoldering parking lot. Eric wished for rain to empty the clouds and get past this humidity.

A shadow moved near his pickup. Eric caught the motion from the corner of his eye. He felt for the Glock kept discretely tucked in his coat pocket. "Alright," he said. "I see you. Come out under the street lamp." The shadow moved closer and entered the lamp's feeble beam. It was Joseph, the first roughneck Eric had interviewed at the oil rig.

"Joseph! What are you doing here so late?"

Joseph's voice was low. "I . . . I had to come and talk with you away from the rig. Others might hear me and speak to higher-ups."

"I'm listening."

Joseph glanced around and lowered his voice even more. "You asked about what I heard when Danny screamed."

"Yes?"

"I heard Danny say more than, 'Nooo.' " Joseph leaned in and spoke almost in a whisper so no stray ear could hear. "I am certain I heard Danny yell, 'Not that . . . Nooo!'"

Eric frowned and asked, "What do you think Danny meant by 'Not that . . . Nooo?'"

"I don't know; but something went wrong up there."

"Was there another person on the monkey board?"

Joseph shook his head. "I don't think so but can't say. When he fell we all ran to him."

"Is it possible a person escaped from the monkey board while all eyes were on Danny?"

"I suppose anything is possible. It was night. With rig lights focused on the pipe, it would be easy to climb up or down and not be seen. Looking up to the board all I can usually see is a silhouette or a reflection off a hard hat."

"Joseph, I think we may be able to eliminate suicide as a possibility, based on what you heard. Foul play might be involved. Anything else come to mind?"

"Not right now. I'll keep thinking."

"Thanks! You've been a great help!" Eric enthusiastically slapped Joseph on the back. Joseph winced. "I'm sorry, Joseph," Eric said. "Does your shoulder hurt?"

"Oh, just a small injury from work is all. The oil field business is not easy."

Eric knew that was true. During his stint as a wellsite geologist he had seen many minor injuries.

Joseph hurried off, and Eric watched him disappear into the shadowy world outside the street lamp. *Why is Joseph so eager to talk? Maybe he values truth more than others I've interviewed.*

In his pickup, by dashboard light, Eric entered Joseph's latest information into his private detective notebook. He kept this notebook in his left jacket pocket; his geological notebook was in the right pocket. Eric smiled as he remembered his private detective and geologist friends who kept their notes in electronic format. Eric considered himself old school, but he wasn't stuck in the past. Field work in both consulting and crime investigation meant exposure to all sorts of weather, so he took notes on weatherproof notebooks that allowed recording field observations in a downpour. There are waterproof electronic devices, but Eric preferred light-weight paper over plastic and metal. Besides, his notebooks never needed recharging!

Joseph's conversation delayed Eric reaching Sarah's house. He drove quickly to make up time in the light traffic. Sarah was waiting at the farm house door, her frame outlined by light from inside. Eric briefly recalled her nice looks and, now with backlighting, her well-proportioned figure. For an instant, he remembered her pleasant kiss on his cheek. He didn't take time to analyze why these thoughts popped into his head. Later he would.

Eric parked and finished a hamburger he had grabbed from the only fast food restaurant still open. He stuffed the sandwich wrapper into a paper sack, tossed the sack onto the floor of his pickup, and hurried to the porch.

"Sorry for the delay. Is anything the matter?"

Taking his hands in hers Sarah said, "O, Eric, I owe you an apology."

"What for?" *I hope this is about her story that didn't match Jean's.*

Sarah led him to the kitchen table where hot cups of coffee and a plate of cookies waited. Eric remembered that, during his first visit, a bare table separated them. They seated themselves and Sarah began, "Eric, I haven't been completely honest with you about Danny and Jean and Bodien." Eric waited without expression.

"I've known Jean since high school. We were good friends; we even attended college together until Jean quit. We've visited many times since. And I knew Danny dated Jean. I introduced them but didn't approve that they dated. Danny always enjoyed a challenge, and he tried to help Jean get her life straightened out, but Bodien blocked the way."

"I see," said Eric.

Sarah spoke with conviction, "I still don't know why Bodien and Jean came to the farm. And I have no idea why someone killed Bodien."

"What about Bodien and Danny? Any connections, besides Jean?"

Sarah shook her head, "Other than Danny crossing him over Jean, no, I don't think so. If something else existed, I didn't know about it.

"O, Eric, I had to straighten out my story with you. I felt awful covering up some of the connections between Danny and these people. I didn't want to cast Danny in a bad light since he was associated with Jean and Bodien. And, just to be clear, Jean visited me after I ordered them off my property."

"Thanks for calling, Sarah. I had a hard time putting together your story and what Jean told me. But I learned something that might move the investigation of Danny's fall forward."

"What ... What is it?" Her eyes widened in anticipation.

"One of the roughnecks heard Danny scream, 'Not that ... Nooo!'"

"Really?" Sarah stared in shock.

"I am sure that rules out suicide as an explanation," Eric said. "I sense foul play. I don't know what happened or who was involved. But now I'm wondering if that note Danny left might be related to his scream."

Sarah sighed in relief. "I knew it couldn't be suicide! Danny was a believing Christian. He had a healthy outlook on life. He was never depressed, and he showed no symptoms related to mental issues."

Eric nodded that he understood.

"What's next?" Sarah looked at Eric with eager anticipation.

Eric thought a moment. "I need to find out exactly who worked that night and if all were accounted for when Danny fell. The whereabouts of people at the rig could be key. I also need to find the harness Danny supposedly wore. I've been so busy trying to get official information that I haven't worked on what may be the real evidence to solve this case."

He stood to go, but Sarah leaned across the table and placed her hand on his shoulder to lightly restrain him. Their eyes met. Eric saw, for the first time with clarity, her beautiful hazel eyes. "Don't go just yet," she said. "I need you to tell me everything Jean said and go over what you know so far. My mind's been in a fog, and I want to know all the details." She moved into the living room and seated herself in a comfortable place on the sofa.

"Please sit here with me, Eric; I need to be near another soul right now."

"Didn't someone from the church come out?" Eric asked as he sat down.

"Yes, but Julie left at 10:00. She had to prepare for a meeting tomorrow. I am usually not afraid, but Bodien's death changed all that."

"I understand." Eric wanted to console her. He reached into his jacket to pull out his notebook and began to read from it. Sarah closed her eyes as she listened and soon entered the early stage of sleep. She slumped onto his shoulder. Eric looked down at her and smiled. He yawned and looked at his watch. 2:00 A.M! He gently placed a pillow under Sarah's head and pulled an afghan over her. Then he slipped over to a large easy chair, collapsed into it, and fell asleep himself.

Chapter 7

*T*he next morning Sarah awoke, stretched, and looked at the form sleeping in her easy chair. She smiled and realized what had happened. Eric was still out, so she quietly got up and went to the kitchen to fix breakfast. Eric returned to consciousness an hour later, rubbed his eyes, and remembered where he was. The aromas of bacon, coffee, and muffins greeted him. "Sarah," he called, "that smells great!"

Sarah had seen him toss the drive-in food sack the night before, and she laughed. "You are just in time to enjoy something other than fast food!"

"Don't mind if I do!" Part way through breakfast, Eric let out a contented sigh. Sarah's culinary skills impressed him. "Sarah, you have made my day." He said this with a smile while taking a second muffin. "I haven't had such a good meal in a long time."

Sarah smiled shyly.

"I've got to get going," Eric said a few minutes later. "There's much to do. Thanks, again, Sarah."

"Thank you, Eric, for staying with me. I think I can manage my feelings better now."

"I'm glad to help." He took his plate and cup to the sink, thanked her again, and turned to go.

Following him, she said, "Eric, please come again and tell me what you find. I'm sorry I fell asleep last night."

"I will. And don't worry about last night. I was exhausted too." He took her hand and gently squeezed it. Sarah reached up and kissed him on the cheek again. Eric smiled and left the Isaacs home with a light heart. As he pulled out of the driveway, he thought this client-private detective relationship seemed unusual. *But I like it!*

Sarah stared after the black pickup and then returned to the kitchen. As she began to clean up, she wondered about this private detective she had hired. *Eric Bonfield. What a nice man. I feel less stress now that he's working on the case.* All she really knew about him involved his professional life. *Does he have a personal life?* She laughed at this thought. She recalled the last time she had been so happy. It seemed a long time ago, but it wasn't. How well she remembered that morning . . . .

* * * * * *

A bright ray of sunlight awakened her from a labored slumber. Sleep had not come easily—not until the early morning hours, and she did not feel rested. Glancing out her window, she saw a cloudless sky. It looked like another warm, humid June day in Arkansas. The bedroom curtain swayed gently at the window, and a breeze stirred the tree outside, but she didn't notice; she was thinking about the day ahead.

Sarah opened the calendar on her cell phone to verify the date. She needed assurance. *Yes, today is the day the oil company representative promised would come. He had said that the drill bit would puncture the Smackover Limestone on my property today.* Her heart began to pound. If everything clicked, her life could dramatically change overnight.

What would it be like to sit on a major oil field? The penetration of a hard bit into porous rock saturated with oil could make her a very wealthy person. Or, if things were not favorable, as the rep had warned, this well might be just another dry hole. "After all, most wildcat wells are dry," he had told her. Sarah knew this to be true from her geology class at the community college.

To keep her mind occupied, Sarah brewed a pot of coffee. When the phone rang, she grabbed it, and said eagerly, "Yes! This is Sarah Isaacs."

"Ms. Isaacs, this is Frank Zietel. I have positive news for you. Arkwell achieved target depth and initial tests look like we have success. Based on the earlier geophysical work, our geologist thinks your land sits on a nice oil field. Congratulations!"

Sarah's brain finally registered what Zietel said. She asked him to repeat it. "Yes, you have a producing well. Royalty checks should be in the mail, so to speak."

Euphoria carried her throughout the day, and she could hardly sleep most of that night either. The following day she watched as a surveying crew carefully measured the distance and position for the next drill hole. The rig moved to a new location. Soon a second well was being drilled on her farm. The typical sound of an operating oil rig resumed. At the same time, workers swarmed around the first well, preparing for production. *They work so fast!*

It was during the drilling of the second well that Sarah had caught sight of a man in the crow's nest on the rig. The man looked like her brother . . . she was sure it was her brother. *What is Danny doing up there?* It looked as if he was working with drill pipes high on the tower while other men worked on the rig's floor. If it was Danny, he stood on a tiny platform as he helped maneuver pipes into position.

Tears came to Sarah's eyes as she remembered her one and only phone call to verify that Danny Isaacs indeed was working on this oil rig.

"Danny Isaacs, what are you doing up there?" she exclaimed. "I thought you worked in a factory!"

Danny scoffed, "Aw, Sis, factory life is so boring. I decided to try something more exciting. I followed up an ad for roughnecks, and I've been doing this for a few months now."

Sarah knew that Danny had always liked to stretch limits. He entertained the family at birthdays and holidays with stories about his latest escapades. Danny's birthday in January was the last time they were together. It was true that Danny never got into real trouble; he just enjoyed pushing the envelope farther than most people. She had never worried much about

Danny; he always managed to wiggle out of tricky circumstances. Now, here he was, perched on an oil rig on the family farm. Sarah asked Danny why he was up there.

She could still hear Danny's nonchalant reply. "It's a neat place to work, Sis. It is called a *monkey board* but we call it the *crow's nest* because there's space for just one person up there. It's a small platform with enough room so I can move drill pipes into the jaws of the topdrive. The guys on the drilling platform do the work of screwing the drill pipe sections together. I help guide the pipe sections. It's hard work, but I like it."

Sarah's sisterly voice trembled with concern. "But, Danny, is it safe?"

"Sarah, don't worry. I've got a safety harness to keep me up there. Besides, it's a great view!"

"But I've heard that oil rigs can catch on fire. What will you do if that happens?"

"No problem," Danny assured his over-protective sister. "I don't know if you can see the wire that runs from where I am to the ground; it's called a *geronimo*."

"What's that?"

"A geronimo is my lifeline," Danny assured her. "If a fire breaks out, I jump on this wire and slide to safety well away from the rig."

"Whew, that doesn't sound like a very safe thing to me," Sarah replied. "O, Danny, I'm worried."

Danny's response was enthusiastic and final: "Well, I want you to know, Sis, this is a very safe operation. I like the people I work with, and the pay is great! Sure beats a factory job!"

* * * * * *

As Sarah straightened the living room, she shook herself from this last memory. Something on that rig was not "very safe", and she desperately wanted to know what happened. Any remaining euphoria she felt for royalty checks had completely evaporated.

Chapter 8

After a brief stop at his apartment to shower, shave, and change clothes, Eric headed for the office of Arkwell Oil's Field Operations. Since the company concentrated its explorations in this part of Arkansas, all company offices were in Little Rock. The Office of Field Operations, like the safety investigator's excuse for an office, was in a rundown strip mall that lacked an attractive ambiance. Also like the investigator's office, the Field Operations office was shabby, with furniture that was old and scarred with use. The walls were a dull green, and the most recent paint job had not covered the previous pink shade. *Another dump! These people don't believe in spending money on administrative quarters.* At least this employee did have a secretary. She led Eric to the field manager, who said, heartily, "Edwin McCloskey. What can I do for you?"

A man in his mid-50s, McCloskey reminded Eric of a hawker at the state fair. His demeanor and speech did not illicit confidence.

"Eric Bonfield, private investigator for Sarah Isaacs. I'd like some information on the oil rig where Danny Isaacs fell. Can you tell me who worked that night?" Eric's identification and papers opened a door to information, and he found himself staring at a ledger of workers and their assignments.

"Looks like six were on site that night," said McCloskey.

Eric wrote the names down and thanked the manager. "By the way, Mr. McCloskey, do you happen to know anything about the safety harness supposedly in use that night?"

The manager shifted his position and coughed. "Well, I don't have information on that particular feature, but I suppose it is still in use on the rig. The investigator didn't say anything about it."

Eric smiled grimly, but said nothing. He left the office despondently. *Why is everything so sloppy at Arkwell Oil? No information about a person who dies on their rig. What are they hiding? Faulty equipment or something else?*

At least Eric knew the names of workers at the site on that terrible night. On his first visit to the rig he had spoken with four men. Danny would have been the fifth worker. That left only one more person to interview, Freddie Farnsworth, the mudlogger. Perhaps Freddie could shed more light. Eric looked at his watch and noted when the shift would change at the rig. He might as well work at the office until he could catch Farnsworth for questioning.

Freddie Farnsworth's shift had just finished as Eric drove onto the drill site. Freddie had long black hair and merry eyes. Eric asked lots of questions but got nothing of substance. Freddie had been in the mudlogger's trailer when Danny fell. Someone pounded on the trailer door and Freddie ran to see what happened. So, Freddie apparently wasn't involved with Danny's fall.

Eric talked with another roughneck coming off work. "I saw Freddie run out of the trailer right after Danny fell," the worker said. "We were all on ground level when Danny died."

So, none of these guys could have been on the monkey board with Danny. Bodien Kessel? Or somebody not on my suspect list. I need to talk with Joseph.

Joseph was wrestling with a piece of equipment when Eric walked up to him. The roughneck paused to catch his breath.

"Joseph, did anyone other than the workers visit the rig when Danny fell?"

After a moment, Joseph said, "Yes, an oil company rep came for a little while."

"What did he do?"

"I didn't follow him. Typical safety inspection. He criticized some stuff and walked around the rig. Then he left, I guess. That's it. His name tag read, 'Murphy Edwards'."

Murphy Edwards: next on my interview list. Eric thanked Joseph and returned to his pickup. Then, on second thought, he got out of his seat and asked to see the man in the crow's nest. George Medly was also coming off his shift. He was a powerfully built man with years of oil field experience. He talked freely. "No problem with the safety harness I used today. I always inspect it myself in detail. Don't trust anyone else to do it. That piece of material is life or death for me."

Eric nodded and asked about its appearance.

"It's brand new. Never used, as far as I can tell," Medly said. "The company replaces them on a regular basis. I doubt it's the one Isaacs used. Old harnesses are sent to a local recycler."

Eric wrote down the name of the recycler and decided that person would be his next call.

Frankie's Recycling was located in a small industrial park on the outskirts of Little Rock. He was lounging in an oil-stained chair by the door when Eric drove up. A jovial man with blond hair and brown eyes that missed little, he greeted Eric enthusiastically. "I'm the sole owner and operator of this here fine establishment," he chuckled. Frankie told Eric that he regularly took in safety harnesses of all kinds. Although a small part of his business, state regulations assured a continuous supply. "Them oil folk is bent out of shape over safety, ya know?"

"Do you remember the harness from Arkwell's rig where Danny Isaacs fell?"

"Oh, yes. I heard about the fall. Very sorry for the family."

"Do you still have the harness?"

"Matter of fact, I set that one aside. Ya never know when some inspector wants to see a piece of failed safety equipment."

"So you consider the harness a failed unit? Why do you say it failed?"

"I'll show ya." Frankie led Eric to a bin in the back room. "Here it is. I marked it so I could find it easy if somebody wanted to see it."

Eric did a quick inspection. "It appears these straps were cut. Is that how it looks to you?"

Frankie nodded, "Yep, that's what I figured when it came in. I wondered why some investigator never saw it." Eric wondered too! Then Frankie observed, "Besides the cuts, the harness don't show no signs of wear. It might have come off the shelf new if it weren't for them sliced pieces."

"Frankie, is it alright if I take this harness for evidence? I have authority to take it to the police."

"Course! Help yourself."

Eric's mind hit high gear! At last, a break that might really be a break! Danny had mounted the rig that fatal night with a brand new harness. It showed no discoloration from use. The cleanly sliced straps were proof that Danny's death could not have been caused by wear or manufacturing error. The inspector's report was correct in saying there was no equipment failure. *Sometimes, it is the unsaid that really matters.*

For Danny to cut the harness himself and then fall to his death strained all credibility. Someone else had to cut the straps since they were in the back part of the harness. Anyone wearing the apparatus could not easily reach that area. But how could someone else get to where Danny was working without the rest of the crew noticing? The case had moved from suicide to homicide with one piece of evidence. Or had it? *Company lawyers can make a plausible rebuttal out of the flimsiest notions.*

Who cut the harness? Eric knew at least two people who were probably around the rig in addition to the regular crew: Murphy Edwards, the company rep, and perhaps Bodien Kessel. Maybe somebody else? It's anybody's guess who might really be involved with Danny's death. *But why kill Danny?* What had Danny done to earn such a deadly response? Who did this and why? Eric's list of suspects was very short. He needed to expand the list or close in on someone.

Chapter 9

*A*fter finishing housework, Sarah busied herself with the yard. Stan had told her to take off work. He was concerned for her mental health after the death of Bodien on her farm. As she clipped roses, she began thinking about that terrible phone call . . . .

* * * * * *

"Ms. Isaacs, this is Frank Zietel, your representative with Arkwell Oil."

"Yes, Mr. Zietel, I'm thrilled with all the drilling going on!"

"I know you are expecting a call to talk about progress on the oil drilling project, but I'm afraid I'm calling for another reason. You see, there has been an accident on the rig."

Sarah suddenly froze. Her mouth went dry.

Zietel continued, "It seems a relative of yours worked on the tower. Is Danny Isaacs your brother?"

Sarah could hardly speak, but she managed a dry gasp, "Yes . . . what happened?"

"Mr. Isaacs fell from the crow's nest."

Sarah's eyes widened as she blurted, "Is he . . . ."

"Ms. Isaacs, I regret to inform you that your brother did not survive the fall."

The phone sank in her hand as Sarah tried to grasp the words echoing in her ear. *This can't be happening. There must be a mistake. I talked with him only a couple days ago. He seemed so sure of himself, but now . . . .*

"Ms. Isaacs, I want to let you know how sorry . . . ." He continued speaking, but Sarah hardly heard him. Zietel eventually stopped apologizing. Sarah could not speak intelligently. The phone conversation ended awkwardly.

Sarah slumped into a chair and stared blankly into nothingness. She was in absolute denial. *Not Danny! It just could not be!* She looked around her kitchen and wished for someone to share her grief. Mom and Dad? They, and now Danny, were gone. The shock hit her like a hammer blow. She had no family to lean on. She was alone. Tears flowed as she cried out her grief to God. Sarah had given her life to Christ, but events beyond her control had been knocking repeatedly at the door, severely testing her faith.

Sarah cried until her emotional well ran dry. Her mind was numb with pain. Her morning coffee turned cold; her cereal was untouched. Somehow the day passed in a dull blur. When twilight faded into night, Sarah hardly noticed. Eventually she fell into bed, exhausted with the pain of her loss.

Before the wretched phone call, Sarah had toyed with the idea of great wealth, although riches had little real appeal to her. Sarah's father had taught her how to live well regardless of finances. He had been a careful farmer, and their family had never known poverty. When she learned her farm might sit on black gold, she was excited but didn't waste much energy or time dreaming about a lavish future. The future was in God's hands, and it would be whatever God thought best.

Sarah was a practical person. She knew how risky the oil business could be. She knew that most people who hoped for a future of huge financial security faced disappointment. In the oil industry, dry holes are common, she had told herself before Arkwell's discovery. Only a few prospects ever struck oil. *Why should I get excited about a long shot?* She had a comfortable life. Her job as a legal secretary paid the bills. Income from renting her land to a nearby farmer provided a nice cushion. The phone call informing her that

Arkwell found oil was exciting, but this did not alter her basic outlook on life.

After oil was discovered Sarah was bothered by a moral question that had popped into her mind following her conversation with Danny. Her brother was working on the family farm for another company. Did she have any financial responsibility to him now that they struck oil? As owner of the farm, Sarah might come into considerable wealth. Danny's familial relationship carried no legal connection to any wealth underground. *"But he is my brother. Doesn't that count for something? Should I talk with him?"* No easy answers showed themselves.

She had asked her boss, Stan, for counsel. "Sarah, you have no legal responsibilities to share wealth with your brother. You are both adults and siblings, but that is it. Whatever you do with any money you earn by any means is up to you." Sarah already knew that but thanked Stan anyway.

Carefree Danny enjoyed checks from his father's trust. He also made good money as a roughneck. If a truckload of cash appeared out of nowhere, he might blow it, just as his father had feared when he made out the estate plan. *Too true; but I don't want to be a scrooge.* After all, she and Danny had grown up together on this farm. *Don't I have an ethical responsibility to do something for Danny if I strike it rich?* So many questions had no answers.

She decided to confide in her pastor, Reverend Daniels. He had performed her baptism ceremony when she was an infant, and she had known him all her life. After sitting under his ministry and teaching from her childhood, she considered him a wise person. She trusted him completely. Sarah explained her concerns, and Pastor Daniels listened intently; however, he offered no insights beyond those Stan had given. It became clear to Sarah that whatever income might come to her was hers to do with as she wished, a fact that made the decision that much harder to make. *Maybe I should set up a trust fund for him, like Dad did.* Just when Sarah was starting to think of a way to solve her dilemma, she received the awful phone call.

Sarah's mind fast-forwarded to the dreaded events that followed Danny's death. She was next of kin, so she had to identify his body. As she drove to the funeral home, doubts and uncertainties such as those she had experienced at the deaths of her mother and father resurfaced. What happened to her family? They were gone. She was the only one left. No grandparents, no parents, no siblings; only a few distant cousins remained. But she barely knew them.

She remembered mumbling aloud, "This isn't supposed to happen. Good people who love God don't experience all these disasters, do they?" How irrational it sounded now, but such thoughts pierced her soul during those dark days. Words from the Book of Job eventually trickled into her mind. She remembered crying out to God, "Why did you pick me out of the crowd to suffer so much loss?" She was dominated by questions that had no answers.

Danny's funeral had been very different from her father's. Sorrow pervaded the service. Sarah's soul was overcome with grief. At their father's service Danny had consoled Sarah, and she remembered the comfort of his arm around her shoulders. Now he lay in the casket. Her friends tried their best to say something significant. "Danny was so young," was the best some could muster. A few brave friends actually said some comforting words. After internment the church supplied a nice dinner, but Sarah wasn't hungry. She didn't feel like chatting idly with those present. She gladly escaped the church fellowship hall to a world of solitude.

Sarah drove home in a daze and parked in the driveway. She walked slowly up the path and climbed the steps to her porch. In the distance she heard the familiar sounds of an oil rig. The noise at first had been an interesting diversion from the rural silence, but now the sound irritated her. Before Danny's death, she had enjoyed watching the interesting scene as workers moved about the rig. All that changed. The movement and noise had become a constant reminder that her brother had died trying to help her become a wealthy person. *Why would I want money at the expense of my brother's life?* As Danny's closest living relative, Sarah received compensation related to his death, which she donated to their church as a memorial gift. It was the possible oil royalties that bothered her most.

In her living room, Sarah stared at absolutely nothing. Except for the noise of drilling, a wall clock made the only sound. The tick followed each tock without any consideration for her grief. She had no family; they were all gone. First her mother had died from a tumor that took her life. Then came the accidental death of her father doing what he loved most, plowing a field. And now, Danny had died—doing what? Making her a rich person? She grew angry with herself for ever having signed the contract.

Eventually her questions shifted away from whys. *What actually happened?* Danny had assured Sarah that he always wore a safety harness. *Had a fire broken out?* There was no mention of a fire. *So what caused him to fall?* Danny did take risks, but he would never do something foolish to put his life in danger. Questions mounted higher and higher until Sarah could stand it no more. She fell into a restless sleep on the sofa as her mind tried to find answers about Danny's fall to his death.

Several days later an Arkwell rep had telephoned her again. "Ms. Isaacs, our accountants will be contacting you with information about royalty checks. Again, I am so sorry for the loss of your brother. I know the success of this drilling project is dim in comparison to the tragedy you face."

Sarah managed a dismal, "Thank you."

Royalty checks, in the mail. Money seemed so unimportant. Her old dilemma of whether to share with Danny now lost all meaning. *What was money without family?* Sarah paced through her house, thinking about grief and wealth. These strange bedfellows invaded her life. *What a weird combination.* She wondered how to handle this odd series of events that so dramatically altered her life.

Sarah found her Bible and turned to the Book of Job. She sat on her sofa and began to read. Then she remembered a Bible study at church where Pastor Daniels examined this book in detail. She rummaged through a folder labeled "Biblical" and found her hand-written notes from that study. With the Book of Job open before her, Sarah buried herself in a study of what might be one of the oldest books in the Bible and one that dealt with the question of why bad things happen to good people. After several hours, she began to rethink her life and reframe the questions she had asked God earlier. The "why" list of questions began to give way to other thoughts that might generate questions with answers.

* * * * * *

Sarah took a good stretch after her time of reflection and flower clipping in the front yard. She picked up a bucket with weeding tools and marched to her garden. After an hour, she surveyed her work. *Whew! That looks much better! Time for lunch!* As she walked back to the house, she began thinking about McBride's referral of Eric Bonfield and how he had entered her life. She smiled and relaxed a little.

Chapter 10

*A*fter Eric picked up the harness, he thought about who to see next. Jean Myers should know why Bodien Kessel had visited the rig on the night he was killed. *Time for another visit.* He called ahead to catch her at home. Jean reluctantly agreed to see him.

She spoke nervously as she fumbled for cigarettes. She couldn't focus and often drifted off whatever topic Eric brought up. Finally Eric asked, "Jean, have you taken anything to make it hard to answer questions?"

"No, I'm just nervous right now. The cops came back this morning and asked lots of questions about Bodien. That's all. I ain't used to all this attention from the law. Makes me queasy."

"OK, let's relax and think about the last time you saw Bodien. What was his state of mind? Did he own a knife? How about a gun?"

Jean seemed to think longer than necessary before answering. Her hands shook, and she could barely hold the cigarette. Finally she got enough control of herself to respond. She recalled that Bodien had seemed upset about something but didn't say what it was. He always carried a hunting knife. She had never seen him with a gun.

She's not telling the truth. "Did he say what he planned to do after you last talked with him?"

"All I know is somebody depended on him. I don't know nothin' else."

"He didn't say who depended on him?"

"No."

"Did Bodien work for anyone?"

"Just odd jobs, sort of like me. Worked for some guy who ran a debt collection agency, last I knew."

"Really? Do you know which agency?"

Jean told him the name of the company and then said, "I need sleep." She wanted him to leave.

Eric thanked her and left. *This lead may be the only truth she told.*

The collection agency sounded like a long shot, but Eric thought something might turn up; unlikely sources could sometimes crack a case wide open. The address was not in a particularly safe part of town. He made sure his Glock rested quietly in his jacket.

If anyone had emptied Eric's jacket out on the floor, they might have been amazed at what tumbled out: a pistol, cell phone, hunting knife, first aid kit, pencil, geological test equipment, sample bags and two notebooks. If asked about this odd array, Eric would say that he never knew what he might need; his investigations took him to unusual places.

The collections office was in an old brick structure that smelled of everything unpleasant. The owner, a burly man with bushy eyebrows and balding head, greeted Eric with a grunt. The cigar in his mouth made understanding him difficult. "Yeah, I knew Bodien. Too bad about him gettin' killed. No, he ain't done a job for several months."

"Why not?" asked Eric.

The manager sat back in his swivel chair and chewed on the end of his cigar. "Bodien weren't dependable. I got to have people who carry through on jobs, ya know? I'd send him out to collect rent money, and he couldn't find the renter. Lots of stuff like that. Had no drive. Got to be hungry in this business."

Eric wondered if he knew other places Bodien might have worked. "I don't know anybody who'd hire him," the manager said dryly.

Eric checked this visit off as a waste of time and left the agency manager munching on his cigar.

Back in his pickup, Eric paused and considered his next move. The cut harness—evidence of foul play in Danny's death—it screamed murder. *Was Bodien the killer?*

Eric drove to the police station and asked to see the investigation report on Bodien's death. The officer in charge told Eric the facts as he knew them. "It's ongoing; no leads yet."

"Could I see photos and your report?"

His previous successes finding criminals had earned him special privileges and allowed him easy access to evidence storage. The officer handed Eric the folder. It contained a few photographs and the coroner's report. Bodien had been gunned down by close-range shots from the front. Four lethal bullet holes completely ruled out suicide. Nothing on the body gave any other clues, and forensic data indicated no evidence of a struggle. A clear-case of bang, bang, he's dead; no questions asked.

Time to visit the forensic lab. His familiar face in forensics gave him perks— techs knew he rarely barked up empty trees. The lab tech on duty nodded as he listened to Eric's questions.

"Well, I did take samples from Bodien's clothes and under his fingernails, but I haven't looked at them yet. Want me to do that now?"

"That would be great if you have time. Could you check with UV as well as polscope?"

"I will do that," the tech said. He was well-acquainted with the way an oil field incident can be examined through use of both ultraviolet light and the polarizing microscope. Ultraviolet light illuminates petroleum liquids. The polarizing microscope examines a specimen between two pieces of Polaroid plastic, making visible some details otherwise invisible to the unaided eye.

As a geologist, Eric routinely used a polarizing microscope to study geologic specimens. His trade demanded familiarity with how to interpret the beautiful colors which jump through the eyepiece as the microscope stage is rotated. This allowed him to identify and classify different minerals or rock characteristics. Forensic scientists and geologists alike use the scope.

Eric waited anxiously as the tech patiently prepared the samples for examination. Using ultraviolet light, he discovered tiny smudges of an oily substance on Bodien's clothing. "I can run a spec analysis on these smudges if you think that will help."

"By all means, I am really interested in the source of those marks." Although Eric thought these samples might match those of raw petroleum or chemicals used in drilling, he dared not suggest this. No use influencing the tech's thoughts.

Examination of fingernail samples under the polarizing microscope turned up fragments of greenish threads under Bodien's left nails. Eric excused himself, dashed to his pickup, and retrieved the cut harness. The tech took samples from the cut portion of the apparatus and compared them with the nail samples. "Looks like a perfect match!" he exclaimed.

"Bull's eye!" Eric couldn't avoid a big grin.

Everything now pointed to Bodien handling the harness in the crow's nest. Eric thanked the tech and asked to let him know any results of the oily smudge analysis.

"Always glad when information helps a case!"

In his pickup, Eric thought about why threads were only under Bodien's left nails. On a hunch, he called Jean.

"Yeah?" she answered cautiously.

"Jean, was Bodien right or left handed?"

She thought a second and responded, "Right, why?"

"Just trying to see what Bodien might have to do with Danny's fall."

"I can't see Bodien doin' nothin' with that!" Jean said angrily. "He got mad at Danny once, but that's all." Her loud voice was unconvincing.

"Thanks, Jean." Eric closed the call. *Jean might wish that Bodien had no connection, but the evidence favored him at the scene of the killing.*

Thumbing a familiar phone number, Eric fulfilled a promise to keep Sarah up to date. "Sarah, I think I have proof that Bodien may be responsible for Danny's death. May I come and talk about it with you?"

Her excited, "Yes!" was a clear invitation.

Driving to the farm, Eric tried to rationalize Bodien out of the picture. Regardless of any alternative scenario he proposed to himself, none worked. Bodien always came back involved in the murder of Danny Isaacs. Thread matches are difficult to explain any other way. But why did Bodien kill Danny? Did this connect with Jean's statement that Bodien had to do something for another person and do it quick? He pulled onto Sarah's driveway; the crunch of tires on gravel announced his arrival. He hurried up the steps and knocked on the door.

Eric's phone call had caught Sarah washing dishes. She hurried to brush her hair and slip into designer jeans and a white top. She opened the door and brightened when she saw him. Eric always dressed business casual with his signature jacket. His hair, unlike hers, was tousled from the wind because he drove with the windows down as long as it wasn't too hot. He loved the smell of the country. City odors turned him off.

She smiled and grasped his hands in hers which were still warm from dishwater. He felt stress drain away when their hands touched. She gazed into his blue eyes and said, with a touch of winsomeness, "Hi, Eric. Please come in. Have you had lunch?"

Eric shook his head and said that he had been too busy.

She led him to her kitchen table, which she quickly covered with tea cups and a plate of cookies while she fixed a sandwich. "Just a minute while I pour tea. Do you like ham or turkey?"

"Oh, turkey is great. Thanks!"

Eric noticed how gracefully she moved. Her motion almost distracted him from his mission. He shook his head to bring himself back to task.

"Sarah, I've got some serious evidence that implicates Bodien in Danny's fall." He described what he had learned since their latest talk.

"The man now on the rig's monkey board says his harness is brand new. So Danny's harness was replaced. The operations manager I talked to seemed clueless about the harness. He thought the one Danny wore was still on the rig. Maybe the evidence was overlooked during the investigations, but I wonder." Eric paused for a breath.

"The match between Danny's cut harness and the fibers under Bodien's left finger nails place him on the platform with Danny. That Bodien was right handed suggests he used a knife to cut the harness while his left hand held the harness." He paused for another breath.

"Is Arkwell Oil hiding something, or is somebody in the company doing the hiding? It would be impossible for anyone to check the harness and not see that it was cut unless the harness suddenly disappeared right after Danny fell."

Sarah listened carefully, nodding her head as she admired this man sitting across the table from her. Maybe he would solve the mystery of Danny's death after all. Her eyes glistened with excitement.

Eric liked to think out loud. Verbal thinkers develop scenarios best when an audience is present, and with Sarah, Eric had an audience. He began another scenario.

"What if someone sabotaged the harness before Danny got onto the monkey board and then replaced it with a new one right after Danny fell? But how does that square with Joseph's witness of the scream, 'Not that ... Nooo!'? That sound requires someone to be on the monkey board with Danny just before he fell, right?"

Sarah nodded and asked, "Could a person sneak up there and shove Danny without being seen?"

"The darkness and lights on the rig could explain why no one was seen." Eric paused, thinking about the people at the rig that night. "Who might have been involved? Not Joseph? His helpfulness removed him from any conspiracy. Merlin described the friction burn on Danny's neck. That left only two more workers, the mudlogger, and the company rep who grumbled about safety. I'm most suspicious about the safety guy but without good reason; I just have a gut feeling. And how did the harness get into the hands of Frankie the recycler? I wish I'd asked Frankie that question." Private investigator work revolves around asking the right questions at the right times. Eric had been so excited to see the cut harness that he forgot this important bit of information.

Sarah was thoughtful. "Eric, suppose Bodien cut the harness. The threads under the nails of his left hand must mean that Bodien held a knife in his right hand; it fits with him being guilty of cutting the harness. That seems easy to prove. But how could Bodien push Danny off the monkey board without a scuffle? I mean, they didn't have a good relationship!"

"The platform is built for one man. But a second person could be on the tower. How else can we explain Danny's scream and the cut harness?"

They went over Eric's notes again and again. Finally, exhausted after hours of discussion, they stopped talking. Sarah suggested it was time for dinner and Eric agreed. He needed a diversion to let his mind process everything.

While Sarah prepared food, Eric tried to relax. But he kept going back to the problem of how Bodien could be in the crow's nest at the same time as Danny without anyone seeing him. That could be explained with the rig lights, but how could Bodien escape without being seen after pushing Danny? The threads under Bodien's fingernails placed him at the scene of the crime.

Jean said Bodien had to do something for someone. Bodien must have been involved with Danny's death. But why would Bodien murder Danny? Had he been paid to commit murder? And then there was Bodien's death! Who shot him? How could Bodien's death be random, way out here in the country, so far from the city and on Sarah's farm? *There must be some connection with Arkwell Oil.*

Eric thought about how a harness is worn. Most modern rigs would follow OSHA regs and require the harness to be put on before climbing to the platform. From what Eric had seen of Arkwell Oil Company, they may have allowed workers to leave the harness on the monkey board and climb into it there. Eric envisioned the platform environment. It might be possible for someone to be on the tower behind the platform. There would be no problem climbing the ladder at any time. Danny might not have seen someone due to the bright lights. If the killer used a very sharp hunting or rescue knife and cut low on the back of the harness, Danny could have been surprised and would not have reacted in time before being shoved. That could explain the burn mark and the fall out of the harness, as well as Danny's scream.

Or could Danny have felt in an especially risky mood and not bothered to check the harness? Had he seen the cut straps? This seemed very unlikely. Then there were the leggings of the harness. *Had Danny neglected to use them because of carelessness?* Eric knew that workers disliked wearing the leggings and occasionally didn't use them. Somehow, Danny fell completely out of the harness. *Was it murder? Apparently. It must have been Bodien. But why?*

Eric couldn't stop wrestling with possible motives for Bodien's death. *Did someone need to keep the whole Danny incident quiet—kill the killer and no witness can point a finger at the instigator? But why kill Bodien on Sarah's place?* If someone wanted to separate Danny's death from Bodien's murder, it made no sense to have both so close to each other. *Had someone messed up and mistakenly murdered Bodien so near to where Danny died?* No scenario for Bodien's death made sense.

Sarah brought a tray of aromatic dishes to the table, and she asked Eric to pray grace for the meal. He did so willingly and added a request for a clear break in the case!

After they finished eating, Eric and Sarah rambled again through the many questions surrounding the deaths of Danny and of Bodien. This eventually exhausted them, and they both stared into space. Finally, Eric said, "Sarah, thank you for helping me think through some possibilities in these murders."

She smiled and grasped his hand. "Eric, I am so pleased with the wonderful work you are doing. I can't tell you how much all this means to me." Embarrassed, Eric patted her hand and said he ought to be going.

At the door, Sarah reached with her hand to touch his face and gave him what seemed to be more than an obligatory kiss on his cheek. From the look in her eyes, he knew she had additional thoughts. He smiled and squeezed her hands. "I promise to do all I can to solve this case."

Driving away from the farm in his pickup, Eric scratched his head and thought about Sarah's hazel eyes that spoke words her mouth did not speak. *I've never had a client like Sarah Isaacs. Never. I wonder if she . . . .* But he couldn't finish the thought. Words stuck in his imagination.

As dusk gathered, he drove toward town and Eric's mind drifted back to his childhood . . .

* * * * * *

His father was an austere man who rarely expressed emotion. He loved his wife and children and worked hard to provide for them, but he seldom showed much physical affection. In contrast, Eric's mother provided the emotional link that held the family together on that level. She helped the children talk about their feelings.

Although he didn't provide much emotional support for his boys, Eric's father believed in education and encouraged them to pursue whatever career they wanted. Eric appreciated that in his dad. After high school Eric enrolled at the University of Arkansas, where he stumbled into a required geology course. The topics opened a whole new way of seeing the Earth around him. No longer were rocks just things to toss into a stream on a lazy Sunday afternoon. Everything he saw in nature started to fit a pattern. Eric's orderly mind found geology mentally comfortable.

A second course focused on Earth history, especially of Arkansas. The landscape of his home state made sense to Eric. He learned that the Earth wasn't just some random arrangement of mountains, rocks, rivers, and plains. The central and northern parts of Arkansas, with their rugged hills, expressed great collisions of continental plates. The southern part owed its flatness to the rise and fall of the ocean, which deposited rocks ripe with petroleum. Everything had an explanation. He was hooked, so he notified the registrar that he had found a major.

The geology program came rather easily for Eric. He took the obligatory chemistry, physics, and math courses. During the summers he worked for a consulting geologist doing menial tasks such as collecting water and soil samples and performing routine analyses. It was a great way to learn the practical side of geology. Before long he graduated from the big U, diploma in hand.

Yearning for more, Eric applied to the University of Illinois' graduate program in geology. Field work and practical applications of geology shaped the choice of his courses. He thrived on the rigor of the program. Four and one-half years later he had earned his Ph. D.

Always intrigued with private detective work, he stayed at the University to study criminal justice during the spring and summer following graduation.

Oil fields were booming in the southeastern states, and in September he accepted a position with a small oil company as a site geologist. In addition to regular visits to oil rigs, he responded whenever called by management or when drillers or mudloggers noticed something that required his attention.

After four years in the oil patch, Eric decided to take a different path. His earlier work with a consultant had enamored him with that side of the business. Consulting appealed to his independent spirit and sense of self-fulfillment. His religious upbringing had conditioned him to think of others and their needs. Consulting allowed him to directly help people.

He didn't go into business for himself to earn more money. Eric left a lucrative career to find a greater sense of fulfillment. He knew that money as an end in itself would prove unsatisfying. As a consultant, instead of waiting for someone in Houston to dictate his next move, he could pick and choose projects that he wanted to work on. His frugal upbringing had allowed him to save enough to launch his business. The time was right to change.

At first, Eric's consulting firm did not move beyond what he could do himself. He sent samples out to labs for analysis, but he did his own interpretations. Eventually, details of running an office took him away from what he loved to do. He needed someone to keep the business paperwork in order. This would allow him to focus on the projects and people behind the projects. Megan, who answered his advertisement for an office manager, proved to be a godsend. Her work was thorough, and she required little guidance. She easily organized the office, allowing Eric time to do his work.

The private investigative business evolved naturally from his inquisitive nature. During slow consulting times, Eric shadowed a private investigator for two years, which was required by the State. He took the Arkansas exam to become a licensed private investigator and attracted clients with legal problems often related to geology.

Local authorities came to rely on Eric's intuition and data interpretations for their toughest cases. He gathered evidence in difficult situations, and his analytical eye often spotted details that law enforcement personnel had overlooked. Sheriff, police, and other state agencies eventually awarded Eric a special status, which allowed him to do advanced evidence gathering and conduct investigations beyond that usually done by private investigators. His fame spread across Arkansas and surrounding states. His ability to apply geological knowledge to solve cases proved invaluable. Even the FBI came to rely on Eric to apply his unique skills in federal cases.

* * * * * *

Arriving at his apartment and worn out by so much mental activity, Eric collapsed into bed. He munched on cookies Sarah had packed for him. It took little time before he dropped into slumber. His dreams were a hodge-podge of mental film reels. Like many dreams, none made sense. Yet lurking in his subconscious was the nagging question about how to tie Danny's death with the killing of Bodien.

Chapter 11

Eric woke up later than usual. "Oh, great!" he groaned out loud. "I forgot to set the alarm! No exercise room for me! I've got to get going!" *Murphy Edwards: here I come.*

Murphy Edwards was the safety officer who had inspected the oil rig just before Danny's death. That day he had seemed very concerned about safety issues at the rig, but Eric wondered if his apparent concern had been a smoke screen. A death immediately after his visit seemed oxymoronic at best.

Edwards' office was in a higher class neighborhood than the previous Arkwell Oil offices Eric had visited. *Must be higher in the food chain!* A secretary ushered him in. "What can I do for you, young man?" Murphy Edwards asked pleasantly. His words were well chosen, but Eric felt that the man bore the appearance of someone in charge and wanted others to know it.

"Sir, I am a private investigator working for Sarah Isaacs on the death of Danny Isaacs at the oil rig on her farm."

"Oh, yes! Tragic situation. Must have really unnerved his sister."

"Yes, it did," said Eric, eyeing the man's reactions to his every word. "I must admit, Mr. Edwards, I am less than pleased with the report of your company's investigation."

Edwards bristled at the remark and a truer picture of his demeanor began to show through. "I'll have you know we run a very safe operation here. My investigation is thorough and I know what I'm doing. I investigate all accidents to the fullest degree."

"You were at the oil rig doing a safety check just before Danny died." Eric stated this as a fact.

Edwards stiffened. Eric played his strong suit and hoped for a crack in the man's story. "I also understand, Mr. Edwards, that immediately before Danny's fall, you appeared quite concerned for the safety of the crew. It seems to be a strange coincidence that someone would die shortly after your inspection."

Edwards jumped to his feet with a flushed face. "I'll have you know that I . . . we . . . run a very safety-conscious organization. I spend a lot of my time seeing to that. If some young whippersnapper decides to jump off the rig, how can I help it?"

So, now it finally comes out! "You think Danny committed suicide?"

"What else accounts for his fall?" Edwards declared. "All safety plans were in place. As far as I know, Mr. Isaacs was well strapped in and 'safe as a pea in a pod'."

"That is interesting, Mr. Edwards. You see, I have in my possession the harness Danny Isaacs used that fateful night. The back harness straps had been cut!" Eric paused for effect. "In fact, the burn on the side of his face was the direct result of his slipping out of the harness and the front straps sliding across his face."

Edwards couldn't speak. His "in charge" guy appearance began to crack. When he regained composure and sat down in his chair, it groaned under his weight. With apparent dejection he said, "I . . . I . . . don't know what to say." There was a long pause as he searched for words. "Why . . . why . . . we've never had anything like this happen before!"

Eric's eyes burrowed into Edwards'. He wanted to expose any holes in the safety inspector's story. *Did I hear a slight hint of guilt?* Eric hoped so, but Edwards' loss for words didn't reveal why he was so surprised.

In the silence that followed, Eric did a brief study of Edwards. The man was a classic middle-management sort, in his 50s, with weight becoming a problem. His thinning hair might originally have been blond, but now it was partly gray.

Shaking his head, Edwards said, "I really don't know what to say, Mr. Bonfield."

Eric answered for him, "For one thing, we can dismiss the idea of suicide. No one cuts a harness to do away with himself, especially those straps in the back!"

Trying to reclaim his control of the situation, he said, "You may be right. What do you suggest we do?"

Eric replied immediately, "A thorough investigation must be made of this whole event. It needs to be treated as a murder. Call in the police."

This unnerved Edwards, "Oh, the publicity would be awful. Can't we do this another way?"

"Not from my view. This is an apparent murder, and murder is a crime in the State of Arkansas regardless how embarrassing an investigation might be."

"I'll . . . I'll . . . call my superiors and let them know of this development. I can't initiate anything on my own," Edwards sputtered.

"That would be a wise thing to do. I'll be in touch." He laid his card on Edward's desk and left.

As soon as the door clicked, Edwards placed a phone call. But, unknown to Eric, Edwards didn't ring any of Arkwell's superior officers. "McCleaver? You idiot!" Edwards yelled into the phone. "That private eye, Eric Bonfield, came in here nosing around. He's got evidence that the death of that kid on the rig was anything but an accident. I thought you had this arranged so we were in the clear. I told you to do away with the safety harness. Somehow this P.I. got a hold of it! I hired you to do a clean job, but you botched this up royally! Now, take care of it or else!" Edwards slammed the phone on the table and reached for a cigarette.

Eric had gotten what he wanted from Edwards. He had shaken the company from its apparent lethargy and now they must consider this as a murder case. But he wasn't done gathering evidence. He must follow up with a visit to the police to alert them of his findings so far.

No sooner had Eric returned to his pickup when his cell phone buzzed. The forensic tech's number popped on the screen.

"Hi Eric. I just finished the spec analysis on those oily smudges. They match a petroleum product used as a lubricant on oil rigs. Does that help your investigation?"

"Yes!" Eric said. "Thanks a lot." This firmly put Bodien at an oil rig before his death. *Closing in.* He smiled.

Eric turned his attention to Sarah's safety. He thought she might need to be alert for any change in activity among oil workers at her farm. No telling what might happen now that he'd stirred the hornets' nest. *I'd better warn her.* He drove to her farm, feeling confident the whole mess could be cleared up soon.

Sarah had decided to return to work so she could get her mind off Bodien's death. But today she was home early since Stan closed the office to attend a convention. She had changed out of office clothes into comfortable jeans and a blue top. She was grateful that her work at the law office kept her mind from dwelling on events that consumed her thoughts. Piles of papers in the office occupied her time, and she relished when they were off her desk and in the mail. Hearing the sound of pickup tires, she knew it must be Eric. She flipped her shoulder length hair back and ran to the door smiling.

Eric didn't wait for a greeting. "Sarah," he exclaimed, "I've been to the office of the company guy who did a safety check at the rig the day Danny fell. I think I shook him up enough so the company will get off its duff and consider this as a murder case and get the police involved. When I leave here I'm going directly to the local precinct and show them evidence I've collected. That way they'll be ready when Arkwell calls. It's also a hedge in case the company higher-ups get cold feet."

"Wow, Eric! That's amazing. Thank you, thank you for doing all this! Can you stop long enough for a cup of coffee?"

"Sure, I love your coffee!"

As they sat at her kitchen table, Sarah could not help looking into his beautiful eyes. Then she blushed when she realized he might wonder why she was staring at him so intently.

Finally, Eric said, "Got to go to the police station to get the ball rolling. Sarah, please be careful in case anything strange happens at the oil rig. Jiggling the hive may get some hornets angry."

"I'll be careful, Eric." Sarah saw him to the door and gave him a prolonged kiss on his cheek. Eric couldn't quite hide the glow from the contact of her lips on his skin but he maintained as much professionalism as he could and squeezed her hand.

"See ya!" he managed.

Eric took his usual route along the rural road toward Little Rock. He hummed as he drove. Things were looking up. Maybe he could close this case soon. Once he finished gathering evidence, it would be the law's job to carry out a detailed investigation and close in on the culprit.

What a beautiful afternoon! No clouds marred the sky. He breathed deeply the fresh country air.

About half way to town, on a lonely stretch of the country road . . . a bullet struck his steering wheel. A fraction of a moment later, the crack of a rifle reached his ears. Eric reacted by jerking to the right, temporarily losing control of the pickup and causing it to careen onto the shoulder. The vehicle jumped a shallow ditch and landed with a severe jolt on all four wheels. The pickup was traveling 55 miles per hour, and he applied the brakes too late. A rock outcrop brought the pickup to a jarring halt, and the airbag activated.

Stunned, Eric assessed where he was and what to do. Pushing the airbag away, he reached inside his jacket for the Glock, while at the same time sliding down in the seat. Whoever had fired the shot had misjudged the pickup's speed; otherwise Eric would be dead right now! He couldn't give the shooter a second opportunity to finish him off.

Eric waited as he crouched low. He barely breathed. All his senses were alert for any movement or sound. The shooter had probably used a high-powered rifle with a sniper scope and had fired from a distance. Would the killer come to see if the shot was successful? Eric was poised, ready if anyone approached. One minute, two minutes, five minutes passed. The only sound was the chirping of a few insects outside his now smashed vehicle. Eric knew that professional killers usually wanted to be certain they had made a hit, so surely someone would come to check. He must not hurry to rise and expose himself to another shot. *That one might not miss!*

Then he heard the sound of a car being driven slowly. The brakes squeaked and an engine chugged to a halt. Eric tensed, holding his gun ready. He had never used his pistol in a deadly confrontation, and he hoped he wouldn't have to now. But someone had tried to kill him.

Why me? The question raced through his brain. *Who would want to do me in?* Oh, evidence he had gathered resulted in criminals ending up in prison. Eric doubted any of them would do something this drastic once he or she gained freedom. Most of the criminals Eric apprehended were not super-violent types. *Maybe the shooter was someone who knew about the murder case.* Eric didn't have time to work this out, as he soon would be coming face-to-face with whoever had parked their car near his wrecked vehicle.

Eric heard the crunch of feet on gravel, followed by muffled steps as the person crossed a grassy ditch.

Then a shout came. "Hey! I'm Jim Englesh! Anybody in there? Anybody hurt?" Eric let out a breath. The voice of one of Sarah's neighbors brought relief.

Eric straightened up from his crouched position and shouted back, "Yes. I'm OK."

"What in the world happened to you?"

Eric shouldered his Glock, cautiously opened the door of his pickup, and looked around. He was shaking from his close encounter with a bullet. Seeing nothing suspicious he replied, "Well, it seems I may not be very popular around here, Jim. Someone tried to shoot me as I was driving into town."

"Really? Shot at you, you say? Are you all right?"

For the first time, Eric examined himself. Except for a few scuff marks, he remained intact. "Yes, I think I'm all in one piece."

Englesh said, "That pickup is not happy right now! From the looks of it, you may have quite a time getting it to move."

Eric nodded. "I wonder if you would mind giving me a lift to town."

"Glad to. Hop in. It's a long way to walk! Do you think you are safe?"

"I hope so," Eric answered. "The shooter must have thought he got me and left. Just a minute while I get some things." Eric retrieved the harness, then he locked the pickup, grateful for a friendly face and a ride.

On the way to town, Eric called the sheriff to report the shooting. Then he called his insurance company and arranged for towing his pickup to a repair shop once forensics had inspected it. Englesh dropped Eric off at a car rental, where he chose a sedan. *I wish they had a pickup; I don't like sedans.*

In all the action of the past hour, Eric almost forgot his mission—the police station. He drove there at once. Craig Wilson, the initial investigating officer for Danny's case, sat desk and had a hard time believing Eric's story of finding the cut harness, since this made the case a murder investigation.

"That sure changes things, doesn't it!" exclaimed Wilson.

"I hope your department launches a full scale investigation into the murder of Danny Isaacs."

"Right! I'll report this to the captain so things can get moving. Any idea who shot at you?"

There had been no time for Eric to reflect on this, so he said, "Well, I've been influential in sending a few bad guys away. Maybe one is out and wants revenge. But that hasn't happened before, and it seems strange this incident occurred right after I discovered that Danny Isaacs' fall was no accident."

"Who else knows about this? About what you found, that is?"

Eric thought a second and then said, "Well, there's the guy at the recycling place, but I can't see why he'd have any interest in doing me in. After all, he seemed glad to help."

"Yeah," Wilson agreed. "I know the guy you're talking about. He doesn't strike me as too likely a suspect."

Eric continued. "Sarah knows, but she can hardly be considered a suspect! After all, she is the one who believed there was foul play in the first place."

"I think she is off the list," agreed Wilson.

"I've talked with other people," Eric said, "but the only ones who know for certain about the cut harness are the lab tech in your forensics section and Murphy Edwards. He was the oil company safety rep at the rig just before Danny's fall."

"I would rule out our tech!" Wilson said. "He's been with us for several years and is very dependable. I don't think he'd tip anybody off."

"I guess that leaves Murphy Edwards," Eric said. "When I left him, he was supposed to contact higher level management in Arkwell Oil Company. Maybe he did or maybe he didn't. I suppose anybody in the food chain might be responsible for shooting at me. It could be almost anyone in the company."

They talked some more, and Eric filled out a report on the shooting incident. Wilson said he would get things moving on a full investigation into Danny's death. "The case is complicated, since there are possibly two murders and one attempted murder. I've never seen one as big as this before. Most of the stuff I see is pretty routine. You know, robbery, drugs, auto theft, illegals . . . stuff like that."

"This could look good on your resume," Eric suggested, planting a seed to speed things up.

"I'll take the harness to evidence storage," said Wilson.

"I was careful not to touch the harness without gloves. Several people may have handled it but that can be determined later."

Eric left Wilson and had a late lunch. Later that afternoon, he went to the repair shop to find the bullet which hit his steering wheel. The mechanic was finishing a preliminary estimate for the insurance company when Eric arrived. "Any sign of the bullet that hit my pickup?" Eric asked.

"Nope, but you can check for yourself."

Eric hoped the bullet might have ricocheted around the cab and come to rest somewhere. He searched carefully, using his training in physics to guess the bullet's movement. Just when he was about to give up, he noticed a small tear in the seat cover on the passenger side. Beneath the tear he found the bullet lodged a couple inches deep in the padding. Graze marks indicated the bullet's lost momentum as it bounced around until it came to rest.

Carefully bagging the object, Eric returned to the police station and handed the bullet to Officer Wilson. "This might be important if grooves on the bullet match somebody's rifle," said Eric. He didn't mention that whoever did the forensics on his pickup had missed it.

Chapter 12

Eric decided he must break the news to Sarah about the attempt on his life. He stiffened when he thought about her. *Is she in some killer's sights too? She knows about the harness.* A wave of panic hit him. He sped to the farm, choosing a different route, just to be safe.

When he arrived, Sarah invited him into the kitchen. "Just fixing a very late supper, Eric," she said. "Can you stay?"

"Sarah, "I've got some bad news."

She stopped her preparations and looked up, startled. "What is it?"

Eric explained about the shooting incident, his talk with the police, and finding the bullet.

Sarah sat down at her kitchen table, stunned. "Who would do such a thing? How did anyone know what you knew?"

"That's just the problem. Everything points to someone in Arkwell Oil's management."

Astounded, Sarah said, "Eric, the representatives who visited me were always pleasant. They didn't seem like the kind of people who would shoot anyone."

Eric's cell phone rang. It was Officer Craig Wilson. "Look Eric, I know this sounds weird, but I've been called off the case. Seems one of my superiors, the captain, wants to head up the investigation. He says it's too far-fetched to be anybody in Arkwell Oil. Says he'll check things out, but to let it ride for now."

Eric's jaw dropped. "What! How could anyone think that?"

"I know you are disappointed, but my hands are tied." Wilson paused, then spoke in a whisper. "I took the harness and bullet before they got into evidence storage and bagged them. Since they were never officially entered in the log book, I thought you might like to keep them, just in case. They are in the trunk of my car if you want them. I know this isn't protocol, but I smell a rat somewhere, if you know what I mean."

Eric could hardly speak, but he thanked Wilson and said he would meet him after work the next day to pick up the bag of evidence. After Eric rang off, he stared at Sarah in disbelief. He repeated the conversation to her wide-eyed gaze.

She stammered, "Why would the police do something like that?"

Eric shook his head. "I have no idea. But I'm going to retrieve the evidence and hide it somewhere safe until this case can be reopened."

They absently toyed with the meal Sarah prepared. Neither was hungry, nor did they know what to say.

Finally, Eric turned to Sarah and voiced his fear, "Sarah, I'm worried about your safety."

"Why me?" Sarah asked. "You are the one they shot at!"

"I know," Eric agreed. "But think about it, Sarah. Whoever knows about me knows that I come here and talk with you. In a worst-case scenario, you may be in danger too."

Sarah's mouth gaped. She stared out the window and wondered. Like all farmers, she owned a gun. It was an old shotgun her father had used. She had practiced shooting with it, and she wasn't a bad shot!

She turned to him. "What do you think I ought to do, Eric?"

"Stay with someone you can trust. Some people from my church will take you in."

"What about the farm? Can I leave it?"

Eric thought a moment. "I don't think these people give a care about your house. They are worried about who can implicate them, or him, or her, in a murder or murders."

Sarah stopped him. "Her? Who are you talking about?"

"Oh, I was just being generic. Anyone might be a suspect. I've talked to quite a few different people." *Jean? She's probably little more than a pawn in the whole situation. But she is on my list of involved people.* "Look, Sarah, I would rather be safe than sorry. Let me call some of my church friends in town. I think you could stay with them for a while. It's better than you being out here alone."

Reluctantly, Sarah agreed. While Eric made the call, she packed a suitcase of essentials and made ready to leave her home. She made a last walk-through of the living room and kitchen. As she surveyed the rooms, Sarah reflected on the farm house that had become her refuge. Everything she saw generated a memory of her childhood years and her parents. Her mom and dad had been the two closest people in her life. Her beliefs, her goals, and her lifestyle had all been developed in this home under their guidance. The house also reminded her of Danny. *Danny.* Tears began to trickle down her cheeks. She wiped them away and resigned herself to whatever changes might be coming in her life. She picked up her handbag, and Eric grabbed her suitcase. He wanted to get her out of danger as quickly as he could.

By now the dark of night had fallen, and there was no moonlight to illuminate the countryside. After Sarah turned on some lights to give the house a lived-in appearance, she followed Eric to the front door. As Eric stepped out onto the porch, he stumbled in the darkness. The movement saved his life. A rifle cracked, just after a bullet missed his left temple. Later Eric wished that the sound of a rifle would travel faster than a bullet, but that would require a change in the physics of the universe. He shouted, "Sarah! Get back!" as he lurched backwards into the house.

A second bullet hit the door frame, splintering wood and sending fragments onto Sarah and Eric. Eric slammed the door shut. "Down!" he shouted. Sarah fell to the floor and began crawling toward the back of the house. A third shot shattered the front window, sending glass flying around the living room. Additional bullets pummeled the front of the house, breaking windows and imbedding themselves in furniture and walls.

The few lights Sarah had left on were broken by ricocheting bullets. The room plunged into darkness. *Where was the Moon?*

Eric found his cell phone and dialed 911. The shooting stopped long enough for the operator to hear what Eric told her. She said, "The sheriff will be on his way."

The shooter must act quickly to finish us off or retreat to kill another day. He reached into his jacket, withdrew his Glock, and waited. He sent Sarah as far from the front of the house as possible. Bullets began smashing into the room again, and Eric tried to make himself as flat on the floor as he could. Minutes passed. Then came the sound of boots on the steps and porch.

A heavy foot kicked the front door, dislodging it from the hinges. For a brief moment, Eric could see a shadow in the doorway. He took aim as the shadow paused just long enough for the door to fall inward. Eric squeezed the trigger, and his shot knocked wood from the damaged door frame just as the intruder lunged forward. Eric fired again. This time he heard a grunt and a rifle discharge. The assailant's bullet barely missed Eric's skull and bounced off the floor, landing in a wall and knocking a picture to the floor. Eric fired a third shot in the general direction of the shooter. Silence followed. Eric hardly breathed. Then he heard what sounded like a body slumping to the floor.

Not trusting anything, Eric remained motionless. He heard no sounds of breathing from the direction of the intruder. In the deafening silence Eric could feel his heart pounding. The distant noise of an oil rig provided an ironic backdrop. The wall clock made no tick or tock; a rifle bullet had silenced it. *Where is the sheriff?*

Finally, Eric heard the squeak of tires on Sarah's driveway. He almost breathed again, anticipating the arrival of a sheriff's deputy. There still had been no sound from the slumped form near him. A deputy dashed up the steps, his flashlight sweeping the scene. "What happened?" he shouted as he stepped over the broken door, his gun drawn.

Eric managed to rise, shaking, to his knees. "The guy shooting at us is over there. Don't know if he's alive or not."

The officer, who identified himself as Deputy Smithson, flashed his light onto the form, still clutching a rifle. The person did not move. "Looks like he's gone!" Smithson exclaimed.

Eric rose to his feet, identified himself as a private detective, and briefly summarized what had happened. Smithson carefully reached for the rifle with a gloved hand and removed it from the man's death grasp. "I'd better get an ambulance out here," he said.

Sarah crept back into the living room. She turned on one of the few lights spared in the shooting spree and drew back when she saw the dead man on the floor. "Who is he?" she asked with a trembling voice.

"Don't know," said Eric. "My guess is he's a hired gunman. The sheriff will find out."

Sarah stared at Eric and asked, "Eric, are you all right? Are you hurt?"

"I'm fine," Eric replied. "He barely missed me twice. I've got wood splinters and glass in my hair and clothes, but I'll take those any day to a bullet!" Sarah smiled weakly and nodded. Wood chips fell from her hair to the floor.

An ambulance arrived and removed the body. The floor was stained where the body had lain.

Deputy Smithson examined the rifle. "This is a high-quality weapon," he said admiringly. "Guess he knew how to use it."

Eric ruefully smiled. "Not quite well enough it seems." The deputy laughed guardedly.

Sarah did not find anything funny about this exchange. Someone had been shot dead in her home. The farm house had been her sanctuary, and now it was violated. She did not know what to say or think. She just shook her head and said, "Look at my house! It's a wreck. Broken windows, door off its hinges, bullet holes everywhere . . . ."

Then she paused and looked at Eric. She took his hands and said, "Thank God you were here when that . . . that person . . . ." She shuddered and began to cry. Eric took her into his arms and held her close. Her warm body helped release some of his own tension. Eventually her sobs subsided, and she looked around the room. "What should I do now?"

"The sheriff's department has jurisdiction in this situation and will need to do a thorough study of what happened here," Eric said.

Deputy Smithson chimed in. "Would I be correct in calling this a home invasion?" He was writing on a pad.

"We were definitely invaded, but the shooting began before he entered the house," Eric said.

For the next hour forensic personnel swarmed over the house, taking statements from Eric and Sarah and gathering evidence. Sarah called her insurance company, and the answering service promised that an adjustor would come and assess what needed to be done.

The house would not be fit to live in for a while. "Now you definitely must live with someone else," Eric insisted.

"Well, at least my bag is packed!" She smiled slightly and looked admiringly at Eric. He coughed uncomfortably and suggested it was time to leave.

Driving away from the farm, Eric took a zigzag route to throw off any pursuers. He tried every trick he knew to shake off possible accomplices of the shooter.

Sarah sat stiff and silent. Eric, sensing her anxiety, asked, "Are you all right?"

"Yes," Sarah said, but her low voice shook with fear. Eric coaxed her to talk. At last she breathed deeply and said, "I've never been in a violent situation like this before, Eric. My nerves are shot."

After a long pause she asked, "Eric, how are you?" Then, without waiting for an answer, she changed the subject. "Have you ever shot anyone before? What is it like to be in a shooting contest with someone who wants to kill you?"

Eric shook his head as he replied, "No. I've never pulled my Glock on anyone and actually fired it. Criminals I've come up against usually surrender when they see a gun. Killing someone is against my very nature and my faith."

He paused before continuing. "I don't really know how I feel right now, Sarah. The excitement is over. I value human life. Regardless how bad some people behave, I don't want to hurt them. And killing that man is starting to weigh on me."

Sarah looked at Eric and said, with tears starting to flow, "I can understand only a little how hard this must be for you. You risked your life to save mine." She was silent for a long moment. Then, with a question mark in her voice, she said slowly, "Eric, who was the killer after? Me or you, or both of us?"

"I wonder about that too. I don't have an answer."

For a while they rode in silence. Sarah's tears ceased, and she dabbed her eyes with a tissue. Lightly touching his arm, she said, "Eric, you are a very brave man. And I respect you for your honesty and moral character. Not everyone would be so up-front to talk about their feelings in such a terrible situation."

Her touch allowed Eric to relax a little. As his tension began to ease, he thought about what Sarah said. *Is her description of me right? If so, I owe everything to my faithful parents and friends who helped shape my early years.* "Thank you, Sarah," Eric said quietly. "You know, I offered a prayer for the person slumped on the floor in front of me."

Sarah squeezed his arm and said, "And I prayed desperately for you during the shooting. I'm glad God answered my prayers the way I hoped."

Eric smiled. He admired this wonderful woman riding beside him. *She really is a strong person! She didn't panic during the shootout.*

Eric stopped the pickup in front of the home where Sarah would be staying. *How long will I be here?* Sarah was grateful to Eric's church friends, Devon and Fran, who opened their home to her on such short notice. She needed this safe house, but she felt like a fugitive on the run. *Why am I running, and from whom? Maybe Eric should be hiding instead of me.*

"Good night, Sarah," Eric said. "I'll contact you by phone. If I come in person, someone might find you."

Eric's statement made Sarah feel both fear and sadness. She gave him an affectionate and, it seemed to Eric, especially long and close hug at the door of his friends' house. "Thanks for saving my life," she whispered in his ear.

Eric couldn't think of much to say, so he smiled and leaned down from his six-foot height to her five-foot-four-inches and lightly kissed her on the forehead as one might kiss a child who had stubbed her toe on the playground. "I will call soon."

A thrill went through Sarah's body and she looked up in anticipation. "Please do. I'll look forward to hearing from you." Her hazel eyes reflected the porch light.

She is positively beautiful, even with wood splinters in her hair.

Fran met Sarah at the door and said, "Hi, I'm Fran. Please come in. You must be exhausted. We have your bed ready for you. A hot shower is waiting right next to your room. Would you like some tea? I have the kind that is so calming when I am stressed."

Sarah thanked Fran and, as she turned toward the door, Sarah looked over her shoulder and gave a wave at Eric's vehicle as it left Devon and Fran's driveway.

Eric saw Sarah's wave and waved back. He nodded to himself and drove to his apartment using evasive maneuvers. His own space welcomed him quietly. He was exhausted. After changing out of his glass-fragmented and wood-splintered clothes, he showered and barely made it to his bed. But tired as he was, sleep came with difficulty. His mind kept on racing between people he had interviewed, the shootout, and Sarah with those hazel eyes. *Her eyes are beautiful.* Finally, he remembered Sarah's prayers for his safety, and with that thought, he fell asleep.

Chapter 13

*W*hen morning dawned, Eric went straight to his office. Megan would be worried about last night's escapade, so he wanted to assure her that he and Sarah were all right. As soon as he opened the office door, Megan bombarded him with questions. "Eric! What happened? The sheriff's radio didn't say much."

She stared as Eric told the story. Finally she said, "Eric, this is a lot more dangerous project than anything I've seen you work on before. Your cases don't involve gunplay!"

"You said it! What started off as a fairly routine investigation is anything but routine. Megan, I need to get my mind off what happened last night. How are our other clients?"

"Most aren't too upset," Megan answered. "I've managed to postpone non-essential projects. Have you visited the lady who runs that small rock shop?"

"Oops, thanks for the jolt! Did you make an appointment?"

"Yes, and she is expecting you right now!"

Eric knew not to wait. He jumped into his rental car and sped to the quartz capital of the U.S.A.

Red-haired Cindy Merkie was lounging by her rock shop. It was really a small roadside stand that her father had started. She inherited the business after his death. She greeted Eric cheerfully and led him to the back of her property where quartz crystals in large veins gleamed in the sunlight. A weed-covered path wandered to a small quarry which Cindy's father had dug out years ago. He had started selling quartz crystals to tourists to supplement the income from his job in town. Cindy was an astute entrepreneur, and she sold her inventory for reasonable prices. But her depleted stock needed replacement if she wanted to stay in business.

"Well, here it is," said Cindy when they came to the edge of a newly-excavated area. Several large, exposed veins bristled with sizeable crystals displaying shiny faces. Red Arkansas clay stained some of the exposed crystals. Eric knew they would be treated with an acid solution to clean off the stain.

After carefully inspecting the quarry wall, Eric declared enthusiastically, "Cindy! These are some of the nicest large quartz crystals I've ever seen. They ought to fetch a good price. Looks to me like you have a great thing going here. I'll guess those veins go way back into the rock. I also bet they open up even more, exposing larger crystals."

Cindy smiled at this and touched one of the gleaming mineral faces.

"If I were you, I'd expand the shop!" Eric continued. "There are enough high-quality specimens to keep you in business for a long time. Do you have good workers who can dig out crystals without damaging them?"

Cindy assured Eric she did and thanked him profusely. Eric felt a warm glow. He loved to encourage small business owners. He knew Cindy would make a nice profit from these new finds.

On the way back to town, Eric mulled over the past 24 hours. At night he had shot a criminal to death, and the next morning he had helped a struggling entrepreneur keep her business going! This yo-yo of emotional events gave him an odd feeling. He hadn't bargained for such extremes when he combined geological consulting with private investigation. Had he made a wrong decision by combining the two? If this is what his life was going to look like, was this really what he wanted? As he thought about it, private detectives, especially with special appointments received from various law enforcement departments, are supposed to detect, but sometimes they have to defend their clients and themselves against criminals. Not a pleasant thought, but life's moments can turn ugly.

He thought about the shooter, now dead. *Why had he chosen crime as an occupation? Had he been an employee of Arkwell Oil, or was he in their management, or was he a thug Arkwell had hired off the street?*

Halfway back to town his cell phone chimed. Eric pulled to the side of the highway and took the call with his notebook in hand. Megan spoke excitedly, "The sheriff's office called with the identification of the shooter. His name was McCleaver, a known hired killer wanted in three states. Police could never catch him. The sheriff said that lots of folks are glad you stopped him. He had carried out at least a dozen shooting-for-hire events. Congratulations, Eric! There may even be a reward coming your way."

After Eric hung up, he sat by the highway thinking about what Megan said. *Is it right to receive a reward because I killed someone?* He had been at the right place at the right time. Plus, for all his attempts, the shooter had missed! Eric paused and prayed for the man's family. *How could I face them?* He wondered about that. *I don't care how awful a life the man had lived. McCleaver didn't deserve to die. But what else could I have done?*

Eric continued to talk with himself, asking questions without answers. He liked finding and following clues, whether for geologic or forensic purposes! He also wanted to stop crime. Too bad it ended tragically for some, as had happened last night. *I hope that was my first and only shootout.* If only.

He returned to his office, told Megan about his visit to the rock shop, and called Sarah at the safe house to tell her the latest information about the killer.

Sarah asked, "Why do you think the man wanted to kill one or both of us? That question has been bouncing around my brain. I don't have an answer."

"I don't have one either, Sarah, but I almost guarantee that whoever hired him is somehow responsible for Danny's death. I don't know about Bodien's murder, though. I'll call when I know more."

She said, "I'd rather be at the office, Eric. I'm bored just sitting here. Your friends are nice, but I want to go back to work." Her first-born personality was showing.

Eric suggested she wait, and the call ended with frustration on both ends of the connection. He reflected on the case. Was he convinced that the murder and shootings pointed toward someone in Arkwell Oil? *Very likely. But who at Arkwell?* Eric thought of the bag of evidence Officer Wilson was holding for him. He looked at his watch.

"Wilson's shift ended an hour ago," Eric exclaimed. "Time to pick up that bag." Megan nodded and turned to her computer. As he walked out to his car, he used extreme caution. Every bush or tree might conceal another killer. A drive-by shooter could be waiting anywhere. Eric realized he was experiencing a reversal of roles. Always before he had been the one trying to catch someone. *So this is what it feels like to be hunted.* Although a bit unnerved, Eric decided to not dwell on the idea. He prayed for guidance and decided he must live his life forward. The outside air was refreshing and nobody fired shots as he drove out of the parking lot. *Nice!*

Officer Craig Wilson lived in a middle income part of Little Rock. His clean, split-level house spoke of care. The landscaping and weed-free lawn declared his interest in making a good appearance. That didn't square with the sloppy job his department displayed when they investigated Danny's death. *What is wrong with administration in that police precinct?* Wilson's squad car sat in the driveway. Eric knocked on the door and Wilson answered. In plain clothes, he looked like any other 30-something in this neighborhood. He showed signs of premature balding, which his cap usually covered up.

"Hi, Eric. Glad you came by. I've been wondering all day why no one is taking this investigation seriously." He opened the trunk and handed the bag to Eric.

"Craig, have you come up with any reasons why you think your superior called you off the case?"

Wilson shook his head sadly, "I wish I knew. The captain in my section said tersely that he was taking charge of the investigation. Said there were other factors involved in the Arkwell Oil Company case. He said he would take your report under consideration; that's cop-speak for, 'Keep your nose out of it', and so I am off on a side road scratching my head. I don't get it."

"It does sound fishy," Eric agreed. "'Do you suppose there might be a connection between Arkwell Oil Company and the captain?"

"You got me. All I know is, whenever there's something going on with Arkwell Oil, a cloud covers everything and our investigations grind to a halt. We're always told to leave it to the company investigator. The captain says we must trust that they know what they're doing."

"So this has been going on for some time?"

"Yes. Ever since Arkwell moved to this area a couple years ago."

"What could be so important about a small oil company that it receives special consideration from the police? Could you check any old reports on Arkwell Oil and see what's up?"

Wilson wiped his forehead with a handkerchief and said, "I suppose I could. I'm on desk duty this week. What do you have in mind?"

"No clue. You might look for any squelched reports. My concern right now is cover-up of a murder."

"I'll see what I can find."

Eric needed to talk out this problem with someone from another law enforcement agency. Everything about the murders of Danny and Bodien somehow pointed in the direction of Arkwell Oil. But local city police seemed powerless or unwilling to launch a proper investigation into the case. Sarah's farm sat at the edge of city police turf. In an emergency it all depended on the agency Sarah called for help. She could get a response from the police or the sheriff in about equal time. In the case of the attacks yesterday on Sarah and himself, the sheriff's office responded to the shooting.

Maybe I should call Sheriff Hansen. Of course, the sheriff's office could be involved in a shady deal, too. Eric decided to chance it, and he phoned Hansen.

An hour later Eric walked into the office of Sheriff Christopher Hansen, a pleasant man in his late 40s. He responded to Eric's questions cordially. On the question of jurisdiction in Danny's death he said, "Well, our department has an arrangement with the city that they can do some fringe work when we are busy. I guess that happened in the Danny Isaacs case." Eric asked if Hansen's office received reports from city police in such cases.

"Yes, we get reports, but we extend a level of trust to other law enforcement agencies."

Eric understood the situation. His problem was that he did not trust everyone on the police force. Or maybe it was just a certain captain who had doused water on the fire of Eric's evidence. Eric and Sheriff Hansen discussed the attempt to assassinate himself as well as the attack on Sarah's home. Clues were few: somebody tried to kill Eric; a thug from out of town shot up Sarah's home. The killer is deceased. End of story. Dead end, literally.

Hansen asked, "Any ideas we can follow up on?"

Eric had some ideas, but he wasn't ready to accuse the police of blocking a murder investigation. "Not yet. Still working on it." Wilson was his only hope. Eric thanked Hansen and left.

The day was almost done, and Eric was almost done, too. He grabbed a quick dinner and sought the solace of his bed. How he wished for some fresh thoughts on Danny's death and Bodien's murder. *Maybe tomorrow* . . . .

Chapter 14

*W*hile Eric worked on the investigation, Sarah stayed at her safe house, but she wished to be at the office, even though it was Saturday. She liked to keep busy so her mind could be occupied. She tried to make the best of the situation. Unfortunately, her days became the height of boredom. Reading occupied some of her time, but inevitably she would remember again those days after Danny's death . . .

* * * * * *

At the funeral, Stan had discouraged her from returning to work too soon. She took his advice. She remembered how lonely it had been, sitting at home alone. She needed to stay busy, but housework occupied very little time. Finally, she called her employer. "I want to return to work, Stan. It will be therapy for me. A paycheck isn't the issue. I just need something to take my mind off Danny's death. I'll work for you as your legal secretary as long as you want me to. I enjoy what I do—I feel like I'm accomplishing something worthwhile. Sitting at home and watching royalty checks from the oil company come in the mail is not my idea of a stimulating experience. Please, don't post a want ad for my position."

Stan had breathed a pleasant sigh. "I'll be glad to have you back, Sarah, but the decision is strictly up to you. I am very pleased with your work."

Even after returning to work, Sarah's days passed slowly, especially the nights. Something kept gnawing at her mind: why had Danny fallen? Had the equipment failed, or not? Nothing made sense. The company rep had assured Sarah that they would make a thorough investigation, and he would let her know the conclusion. The report, when it came in, concluded, "There was no equipment failure." She was not appeased; she must know what happened. When she called the company rep to learn more, he repeated that the equipment had not failed. Beyond that he could say nothing.

This lack of information infuriated Sarah. What were these oil people saying by not speaking it? Were they hinting that Danny had committed suicide? *No equipment failure?* That meant the company placed the blame on Danny, who, everybody knew, liked to take risks. But Danny used the safety harness; he had told her so himself. Her brother worked from the crow's nest, and yes, he had quipped that he enjoyed the view, but he also said that he took precautions; he had to. *Danny commit suicide? Never! He enjoyed life.* Things did not add up. The whole thing made no sense. *What can I do to find out what really happened?* Fitful sleep plagued her nights.

Sarah remembered the day she had first contacted Eric Bonfield. She heard about him in her geology course at the community college. Her professor had talked about someone with a double occupation: geologist and private investigator. She found her old school directory and scanned it for her prof's number. Then she grabbed her cell phone.

"Hello, Professor McBride? I'm Sarah Isaacs. You may not remember me. I took your geology course last spring and you talked about a private detective-geologist that you admired. Remember?"

"Oh, yes," said McBride. "His name is Eric Bonfield. Quite a guy. He's got one of the most interesting jobs I know of. He's a consulting geologist with a Ph.D. from the University of Illinois. And he runs a private detective agency on the side. As I recall, the agency has one employee— himself!"

For the first time since she could remember, Sarah felt a glimmer of excitement. "Do you know how I could contact him?" Sarah heard a rustle of papers in the background.

"Yes, here it is. Eric Bonfield lives in . . . . " He read her the address and phone number.

Sarah said, "That's not far from here. Thanks so much, Professor McBride!"

"Glad to help. But, Sarah, do you mind if I ask why you want a private detective-geologist?"

"It's about a death I want to investigate or rather have someone investigate," Sarah replied. "Do you think Dr. Bonfield takes such cases?"

"Well," he said, "I think he takes anything that interests him. It's worth a try."

Sarah felt herself beginning to move out of the doldrums. At last there might be some straw she could grasp to solve the mystery behind her brother's death. Breathing a prayer, she placed a phone call to Eric Bonfield. She was disappointed when a synthetic voice responded. She left a message, wondering if he would return the call.

A few hours later, Sarah's phone rang. "This is Eric Bonfield. Is this Ms. Isaacs?"

"Yes, Dr. Bonfield, thanks for returning my call. There's been a death in my family I would like investigated. It took place in an oil field and I thought you, being a geologist, might be able to find out what happened." Eric listened to the story as Sarah unveiled the details. Finally, Sarah fell silent except for, "Well, what do you think?"

A pause in the conversation finally ended. "Sounds like an interesting case. Before I agree, though, I'd like to talk with you in person and perhaps visit the rig."

They set a time to meet the next day. Sarah's emotions began to soar. She could not wait for this possible answer to prayer to walk into her home.

That had been her first encounter with Eric Bonfield and the beginning of a process to find answers about her brother's untimely death.

* * * * * *

Sarah roused herself from playing her memory recording. *That's enough history. Eric is on the case and I feel so relieved. And he is some man!* She collapsed on her borrowed bed with a dreamy look in her eyes.

Chapter 15

Sunday's sunshine peaked through the window and Eric knew he really needed a worship experience. Focusing on the murder case was draining. Sarah also wished the same, so she went to church with Devon and Fran. Sarah saw Eric sitting with a group of men on the far side of the sanctuary. She smiled and waved. He waved back. Still concerned for her safety, Eric didn't want to draw attention to where Sarah was staying, so he kept to himself the rest of the day. He was surprised how much he missed being with her. She really missed him.

Monday morning Eric decided to visit forensics again. That department had escaped the thumb of the reluctant police captain. The tech asked, "How can I help?"

"I'm interested in Bodien's death. Any bullets or casings recovered from the scene?"

"Whoever did the shooting took a lot of care not to leave casings behind. Most of the bullets passed through the body, but one lodged in Bodien's spine. The others were not recovered." He pointed to the slug sitting in a tray.

Eric produced the bullet fired at his truck and bullets fired during the assault, "Could you check to see if the weapons used to fire these bullets match Bodien's bullet?"

It didn't take long for the tech to compare specimens. Bullets from the dead assassin's gun matched the one used in the attack on Eric as he was driving. And the bullets that had killed Bodien came from the same make of weapon as the others, but not the exact rifle. The similarities of the weapons suggested a common source for the guns. *Is there a stockpile of rifles used for murder by whoever hires the killers?* If so, that further suggested an organized approach to killing people who, for one reason or another, interfered with someone's master plans. Perhaps it simplified things a little. If only the deceased assassin could talk.

Eric felt the urge to call Sarah and catch her up on what he had learned, however pitiful the results. She answered her phone. Sarah's voice radiated pleasure at hearing his. She listened and thanked him for the new information. "I miss you," she said.

Eric flushed at her soft, pleasing voice. "Well, er, I hope you won't have to stay away from home too long." *What else can I say?* He closed the connection.

He felt a growing attraction to Sarah. He found her quite winsome. *Get a grip! I know not to get emotionally involved with clients. After all, Sarah is very alone after the death of her last family member. She needs someone to fill a huge gap in her life. Am I just that; a space filler? No! I am her employee. Period!* Although he thought this, he shook his head. *Who am I kidding?* Here he sat, employed by a beautiful woman who also is a wonderful, spiritual person. So, what's the problem? He smiled broadly and nodded slightly.

Eric had never married. He dated girls in high school and college, but none held his interest. During his early professional days the pool of likely candidates shriveled. His work didn't provide much female contact. Oil rigs are male-dominated environments. Even now, he didn't often see women. His church contacts included eligible females, but most were either too young or much older than he. They were friends, but none could be called his type. *What is my type? Am I too picky? My list of admirable qualities in a woman can't be that long.*

His training at home and church had taught him to consider spirituality a key factor in choosing a life partner. He had seen the results of people who ignored spiritual values and chose mates for trivial reasons. Eric appreciated beauty, but he knew real beauty resided deep inside a person.

93

Moral and character aspects stood high on Eric's agenda. He liked thoughtful people; not flighty ones. He didn't maintain a written collection of attributes he admired in a woman, but he recognized good qualities when he saw them. *No, I'm not picky; I'm—well—selective.*

People liked Eric. Making friends had never been a problem; however, developing a relationship was more difficult. It was this very barrier that had begun to come between him and Sarah. He wondered how he should proceed. *If anything develops between us, I have to be more than her employee or protector.* Eric sighed. *Life can be complicated!*

Eric's phone jolted him from his thoughts. It was Officer Wilson. "I think I may have something for you. Can you meet me at my house after work?"

Of course he could. Maybe Wilson had a chisel to help crack the case! A realistic optimist at heart, Eric believed things would eventually work out. The rest of the day might be a little brighter. A phone call can modify a little melancholy.

Arriving at Wilson's home later that day, Eric saw children playing in the yard. A boy and two girls of elementary school age were tossing a ball back and forth. The ball rolled to Eric, and he threw it to the closest girl. Eric wondered what it would be like to be a father. Having a family would be nice. *Children? Am I too old? And Sarah, is she . . . . Wait a minute, where's this self-conversation going? Do I really consider Sarah someone to . . . .?* Before he could finish his thought, Wilson came to the door.

Wilson invited Eric inside and introduced his wife, a pretty blonde with a bright smile. Eric was reminded of Sarah's silky brown hair, smooth complexion, and winsome smile. Smiling was something she did more of now that the investigation showed some progress. *Got to get Sarah out of my mind. I have work to do!*

He and Wilson sat at the kitchen table in a room where the delicious aromas of a supper being prepared filled the room. Eric's mind momentarily drifted to Sarah's kitchen and the wonderful meals she had prepared for him. He shook his head to clear out such pleasant thoughts. Wilson was talking, but Eric had missed the introduction.

". . . So, I dug a little deeper and, sure enough, name after name kept coming up. You won't believe the number of complaints by disgruntled employees working for Arkwell Oil Company," Wilson said.

Nothing too surprising there. It didn't strike Eric as a place he'd want to invest time. Then Wilson compared the reports of unhappy Arkwell employees with a list of persons who were reported missing during the time Arkwell Oil was drilling in the area. That landed a hit. The list of disgruntled employees and the missing persons list were identical. It was obvious that whoever complained suddenly disappeared.

On top of this, Wilson's search turned up complaints from farmers who had leased land to the company. Something strange kept repeating itself. Leases were signed, geophysics crews showed up, favorable promises followed, and oil rigs drilled supposedly successful wells. More drilling poked holes in farm fields. Then, after a few royalty checks entered rural mailboxes, payments stopped. Arkwell Oil declared the wells were not as profitable as anticipated. Farmers ended up with plugged wells and Arkwell moved on. Duly noted complaints to police never went further than a dead file. Nothing illegal could be proved. Eric massaged his chin as he considered the events that kept repeating themselves.

"What do you make of this, Eric?" Wilson asked.

Eric said, "I'm not sure. I know you are not allowed to work on this case, so I'll talk with the affected landowners."

The men discussed the findings for more than an hour but gained few new ideas about how all the data fit together. One thing was for certain: the whole operation smelled of rotten fish.

Eric thanked Wilson for his thorough work and asked him to keep his ears open for anything new making its way into police headquarters. Eric declined an invitation to dinner, since he was in a hurry to return to his office and do online searching. He would pick up some fast food on the way. It was long past closing time, so he would have the office to himself.

Megan was a great office manager but she only stayed after hours when he really needed her expertise.

As a former oil geologist, Eric had insight into any strange situations that might occur with land-leasing for petroleum, drilling, and production. He knew that oil fields play out after a while. He also knew that only a fraction of oil underground can be extracted without extra effort and expense. Fracking technology allowed more efficient extraction, if appropriate. The Smackover Limestone formation often yielded to this method.

But, sooner or later, cost/benefit ratios favor shutting down wells and moving on. The frequency and repetition of Arkwell Oil's quick in and out operations were anything but normal. Oil fields usually don't play out so quickly. The company either has a habit of hiring totally incompetent geologists or something much worse is underfoot.

A great deal of information about Arkwell leases poured from the web. Nobody but Arkwell worked this part of the state, which just happened to lie within the law enforcement web of the Little Rock police. *Sounds too convenient.* An oil patch is a competitive league to pitch in, so if great quantities of oil lurk underground, why aren't other companies searching the same territory? He understood that big oil didn't bother with small pickings; they left that to midget fry who could afford to work low production fields. But why weren't other small oil companies interested? And was production really limited to a narrow area near Little Rock? *I don't believe it for a minute.*

Eric plotted leases using GIS (Geographic Information System) software and found they followed some sort of trend. *Depths to target* could prove informative. All those listed were fairly shallow and claimed to bottom in the Smackover Limestone. Eric knew that the Smackover was a reasonable target with potential for being a prolific oil producer, so why had Arkwell's wells dried up so soon? Eric studied data that Arkwell had submitted to the state. The reported depths seemed reasonable.

Then he looked at the drilling times that Arkwell claimed that their wells penetrated the Smackover and his eyes widened. *Wait a minute! These times are impossible!* Drills don't reach that deep so fast! The drilling times and the reported depths made no sense. Smackover depths should have taken much more time for this part of Arkansas.

OK, what are the options? Did Arkwell drill to shallower depths through ignorance? That seemed unlikely, since they had geophysical data to predict proper depths. Or did they skip using the seismic information? Maybe they hit a target other than the Smackover, and it was a case of mistaken identity. Or did they intentionally look for a shallow target, but always logged it as Smackover? This company's work was very strange. How could it stay in business with such sloppy work? Who did they hire to do the geological investigations? Or was something sinister going on?

Eric looked at his watch. *Time to close up shop; I am exhausted.* Megan's stack of work for him, which still stood by the computer, would have to wait. Eric logged off, turned out the lights, and headed for the door. Then he felt checked.

Have you forgotten about the mark of death on yourself? Just waltz out onto the parking lot at night without a care in the world? Think, Eric, think! Got to be more cautious. He turned lights back on and exited the back door, careful not to backlight himself and provide an easy target. He approached his parking lot from the side of the building. Things seemed quiet enough, but lack of sound can be deceiving. Eric pushed the remote door unlock as he ducked low and made a dash for the rental car. Sure enough, a bullet whizzed over his head. Eric jumped into the driver's seat, started the engine, and peeled out of the lot.

"This is getting old," Eric mumbled to himself! "Whoever is financing my demise must have serious cash to hire hit men! And they have patience. I spent at least five hours in my office. That's a long time to wait for a shot. Don't these gunmen have anything better to do than wait for me to show? I must have some price on my head!"

Speeding away, he said aloud, "Why did I take this case, anyway? Aren't there other private investigators more qualified to deal with violent criminals?" No more shots came his way. "Guess the killer wanted a sure hit instead of shooting randomly." He called Little Rock police to report another shooting. *They need to know how dangerous it is, at least for me! Maybe they can find a rifle shell when they search the bushes around my office parking lot.*

Reflecting on his would-be assassin's tactics, Eric voted against going to his apartment. Jorge, a friend, could put him up for the night. Making sharp rights, then left turns to throw off tailers, Eric made it to Jorge's apartment without incident. He had called ahead and Jorge sat on his porch waiting to let him in.

"So, what are you up to now?" Jorge asked. He and Eric had survived the University of Arkansas together.

"Let's just say somebody must have a contract out on me, and it is unnerving," Eric replied. They talked for a while. Then, after a brief call to Sarah to let her know of tonight's shooting incident, Eric fell asleep on Jorge's couch.

The next morning, Eric called Sarah to check on her isolation.

"I am bored stiff," she said. "Your friends are very kind, and I'm helping with the house, but I want to return to work. My boss understands, but reports are piling up on my desk. There's an office to run, and an attorney can't wait long. I don't want to wreck his clients' lives because of . . . whatever it is I'm supposed to be afraid of."

Sarah's emotional plea hit Eric in the chest. "OK, I'll pick you up at 8 and hope I am just being overly cautious."

"Thank you, Eric!" Sarah almost jumped through the phone to hug him. Eric shook his head. He feared for her life, but everything pointed to his. Maybe going back to work might be safe enough for Sarah.

Sharply at 8, Sarah walked through the door of the safe house and into bright sunlight. She wore a smart white top and dark skirt. To Eric sitting in his car, she seemed to glow in the rays. He sighed. *She really is beautiful.*

She ran to Eric's car, but instead of entering at the open door he offered, she wrapped her arms around his neck and planted a huge kiss on his surprised lips. The embrace that followed awakened feelings in Eric he rarely had experienced. *Who is this wonderful woman with her arms around me?*

Shaking the thought, he said, "We'd better get going. It isn't good to be seen like this." Sarah laughed and Eric caught the humor in his statement.

When they arrived at Stan's office, Sarah leaned across the seat and kissed Eric again. As she did this, Sarah gave him a look that melted any frost on his emotions. He stammered, "Well, I'll see you at 5 then?"

"I certainly hope so," she said dreamily.

Stan welcomed her back with an excited handshake and asked about the investigation. After a brief update, Sarah plunged into the pile on her desk. She relished the change from inactivity.

By the end of the day she had caught up on her work. She waited eagerly for a glimpse of Eric's car when the church bell downtown rang five o'clock. Sarah lacked the foreboding Eric owned. After all, bullets only seemed to be aimed at him.

Eric hustled her from the attorney's office to a distant restaurant for dinner. Business-like, he caught her up on his day, going on and on about Smackover Limestone, well depths, time of drilling, and other details. She grew tired of the technical chatter but kept a game face throughout his litany. Finally, she grasped what he was saying.

"So, you're saying these people have been lying about how deep they drill their wells?"

"You got it!" said Eric.

"Why would they lie about well depths?"

"That is just the question I'm trying to answer. Do you remember the first well they drilled on your property? Completion came so fast they couldn't possibly have reached even to half the depth to the target they told you about. Right now I'm trying to find which layer they are hitting. I think it is a porous sandstone with no oil at all!"

"That makes no sense, Eric. They told me they found oil and checks would be in the mail, eventually."

"Received any checks yet?" Eric looked at Sarah intently.

"Well, no, I haven't! But a lot of big tanker trucks come and go. At least they did when I was at the farm."

99

"Did you notice anything peculiar about them? Any clue might help."

"Not particularly, but I'm curious about one thing."

"What's that?"

"They seem to arrive more slowly than they leave."

"You mean the tankers leave faster than when they arrive?"

"Yes, at least that's the way I remember."

"Sarah, I think you may have discovered something. Empty trucks move faster than ones that are full. So did trucks arrive full and leave empty? If they carried crude oil from wells, that makes no sense at all. But suppose they brought fluids to the rigs. That could explain what you observed. This would not be odd, except for the other unusual activity by Arkwell. If the wells were not producing yet, then the tankers might leave empty. If this was so, then there should be no checks in your mailbox. We won't know this until we return to your farm and see what's in your mailbox. I have to find out what is going on at your farm." *Arkwell Oil Company, what is your game?*

Eric took Sarah back to Devon and Fran's home and wished her good night. She thanked him for letting her go back to work and gave him a hug. Her embrace was longer and involved closer body contact than would be expected of mutual friends or an employer and employee.

As Eric left, his mind returned to the mental list of qualities he valued in a woman. How did Sarah measure up? *Wait a minute, this is ridiculous. Got to get myself together! Some killer-for-hire may be tailing me right now.* He returned to his "ditch the tail" routine to take his mind off Sarah. Then he smiled to himself. *How likely is that?*

Back home, he dropped in bed and turned off the day as best he could. Yet, for some reason Sarah drifted into his dreams. They were pleasant dreams.

Chapter 16

Days dragged by ominously. Things were overly quiet with no more shots fired in Eric's direction. *Have they given up trying to kill me? I don't know how to proceed on the Arkwell investigation.*

Eric spent most of the time catching up on geological consulting. Many of his clients' problems seemed fairly simple. He eliminated most of Megan's stacks on his desk and those she left jamming his computer. It would be up to her to send out reports, in addition to making the usual phone calls and filing pages of data. No problem there; Megan loved her work. Eric couldn't quite call her a workaholic; she was just very efficient and felt good about what she did.

Sarah was chafing at the bit to get back to the farm. She kept pressure on Eric. "Maybe I'm not a target after all," she said. "Hey, whoever *they* are, they know where I work, and nobody's shot up the law office yet! The sheriff's investigation found nothing new. My insurance company has paid for repairs to the house. I want to go home, *now!*" She could be forceful, and this first born characteristic kept showing itself.

Eric agreed, although with reservations. On the way from her work to the farm, Sarah bubbled with excitement. She asked lots of questions, especially about him. Eric felt interrogated, but he liked talking with Sarah. She was pleasant company and nice to look at!

As they approached her farm, a large tanker truck pulled onto the makeshift road leading to the first well. It traveled very slowly. Going the opposite direction, another truck moved much faster as it left the farm.

This verified Sarah's observations. Entering trucks carried something which remained on the farm. Eric's most generous explanation assumed that fluids were needed to pump into wells to enhance production; but he wondered if production existed. That question could be answered by recorded data and should show up on royalty checks.

Pulling the handle on Sarah's mailbox seemed to answer the question. In the mail that poured out were a number of royalty checks. *Maybe this operation is legit, but why are no trucks leaving with a full load?*

The nicely restored house welcomed its absent owner. Sarah gave a sigh and nodded her head in appreciation. She threw her arms around Eric and planted another huge kiss on his lips! He didn't know what to do, so he enjoyed the moment. Eric's arms didn't quite find their way around her body, although he wished they had; instead, his arms hung limp at his side. *Professionalism, what a drag!*

"Oh, Eric," Sarah cooed, "I so appreciate you and all you do for me."

Eric blushed profusely, stepped back, and said, "Well, you haven't seen my bill yet!" They both laughed. Then they made eye contact. She stared deeply into his irises. Eric blinked first and looked down at his feet; the moment of intimacy had broken. She said it was time to eat; would he stay? How could he resist? Sarah prepared dinner from what she found in the pantry and freezer.

After their meal, they sat on the porch and watched the comings and goings of tanker trucks. Eric wondered if this oil field was actually producing what those royalty checks indicated. Since Arkwell Oil was drilling wells at a furious rate, why weren't large oil companies interested in this field? And why did the tankers leave empty? As evening moved toward night, Eric asked Sarah, "Are you certain it's all right for you to be alone? I mean, it's a mile to the nearest farm."

"No one shot at us today!" Sarah laughed, breaking the serious moment. "Besides, I have my shotgun!" She said this with a grin.

"I'll come whenever you call."

"And I'll take that as a wonderful promise." She smiled bewitchingly.

Their first good night kiss lasted longer than Eric imagined any casual client might give her employee. This time he held her waist. *Was this woman for real?* He hated to leave, but he did.

Daring fate, Eric drove his normal route home without incident. *That was easy. Praise God!*

The night brought fitful sleep, alternating between dreams of Sarah and unknown assailants taking potshots at him. He awoke early and decided to revisit Jean Myers. Maybe a fresh wrinkle would present itself.

Jean was her usual unpleasant self. She wore a faded shirt unbuttoned too low and tight, torn shorts. She smoked one cigarette after another. When Eric asked if she had thought any more about Bodien's final hours, she offered nothing new. "How about Bodien's work other than the collection agency?"

She told about some of his jobs: janitor, gas station attendant, and bouncer at a bar.

"Did he have much money?"

At this she brightened. "Bodien was a big spender. He loved to flash his cash around. Made him feel important, I guess."

"Where do you think he got his money?"

Jean thought about his question a bit too long, but eventually said she didn't know. She knew he paid rent and other expenses in cash. Where the money came from didn't matter to her.

Eric asked, "Do you suppose Bodien had a secret employer you didn't know about?"

"He could have. Some nights when he didn't show up I'd get mad. Then he'd come back and flash money around; so I forgave him!"

"Do you have any idea where he went or what he did?"

"Out of town; said he had things to do."

In a flash of intuition Eric asked, "Did he ever return sort of beat up? You know, like he'd been in a fight or something?"

Jean said he often showed up at her place with a scratch on his face or bandage on his arm. She didn't think much about it, but it happened quite a bit.

"And he returned with cash on those occasions?"

"You bet!"

"Do you think he traveled out of town very far?"

Jean answered too quickly, "Don't remember."

Eric felt better about this interview. *Sometimes you have to ask the right questions.* What is important to one person may lie dormant in the memory of another. *But I don't trust all that Jean says.* Those shifty eyes betrayed something.

After Eric left Jean, he decided to do some snooping at Bodien's apartment. Jean had given him the address. The landlord seemed typical for that part of town: torn undershirt, sloppy and stained pants, a balding head, and a soggy cigar.

Eric asked the landlord if he had rented the apartment.

"I ain't been near it. Too superstitious, I guess. Why? You want to rent it?"

Eric identified himself. "No, but I'd like to look it over if I could."

"No problem. The police already been there."

The man led Eric up three flights of sagging stairs. He unlocked the door, such as it was. "Help yourself. I got to get somebody to clean it out sometime." The landlord left the key with Eric.

Eric surveyed the room. Untidy would be a compliment for Bodien's apartment. Trash littered the floor. *Maybe there's something in this mess the police missed because they didn't know what to look for.*

An hour later, after turning over every piece of paper and fast food wrapper, Eric found the object of his search. Tucked inside a slit in the almost-collapsed mattress was a dirty envelope that held names, addresses, locations, and a fist full of $50 bills. What a treasure trove of information! Eric left the dingy apartment with the envelope in tow. He returned the key and asked the landlord if Bodien owed any rent.

"Yeah, about 100 bucks." Eric fished out two 50s and handed them to the man, who about dropped his cigar. He thanked Eric excitedly.

In his vehicle, Eric thought about how to proceed. Then he started the engine. *I'll need to explain this money situation to the police but not until the case is reopened. I guess this falls under my responsibilities as a preferred P.I. If Wilson's suspicion is correct, this cash could disappear in Precinct #2 and never be reported.*

Back at his office, Eric put the cash in a safe, as evidence. Wilson's captain might suppress the information, so the police would have to wait to see this pile of money and list of names.

Eric carefully studied the names and locations on the list. His breath became short as he started lining up the names in Bodien's envelope with the names on Wilson's list of missing Arkwell Oil employees. A perfect match! Eric could hardly believe it. Everyone on Bodien's list showed up on the police list! Bodien had crossed-out all the names. Eric shuddered to think what crossed-out names might mean. *Was Bodien a hit man or muscle man for the company?* Arkwell Oil became scarier by the minute.

That evening Eric drove out to the farm. Inside her house, Sarah pulled him down to sit beside her on the sofa. She was eager to talk about her day at work. She had been on top of everything, and she loved every moment. "So, Eric," she said, looking into his eyes with more than a casual interest, "How about your day?"

"I think I know how Bodien fits into this picture."

"Really? Tell me," she said, sliding closer.

"Sarah, please! I have some really chilling things to say." She backed away, a bit hurt.

Eric described his visit to Bodien's apartment, how he had found the stash of notes and money, and how the names on Bodien's list matched the names on the police records.

Sarah sat up, shocked. "Do you think Bodien murdered all those people?"

Eric said, "I know it looks frightening. But I can't be certain those people are dead. Maybe there's another explanation."

Sarah shook her head in disbelief. "But if Bodien did whatever he did to those people, why would someone kill him?"

"That's the piece I can't figure out," he said. "Can you help me think of some possibilities?" Eric drew out his notebook and began a litany. "Perhaps the killer was jealous of Bodien's success with the company. That's one possibility. Or the company thought Bodien knew too much and needed to be silenced. Or maybe Bodien tried to shake down his employer.

"Or think about this one, Sarah. If Bodien killed Danny, maybe he felt bad about what he did to your brother. Perhaps Jean badgered him and Bodien felt remorse. That could lead to a breakdown and confession. The company couldn't have that. Maybe Bodien was muscling in on the shooter's girl-Jean, perhaps? Hmm. I should ask Jean if she has a secret beau.

"So, Sarah, what do you think?"

Sarah thought a few moments before responding. "What if Bodien was supposed to take out his killer and the tables got turned? That's another possibility!"

All this thinking exhausted them both. Eric looked at Sarah and she looked back at him. Their eyes seemed to penetrate each other's souls. They slid closer. Soon they found their arms wrapped around each other and they sank into the sofa. *What am I doing? This woman is my client!* Then their lips locked and he temporarily forgot she paid him to come here.

Just then a noise outside jostled them back to reality. Rapid knocking rattled the new front door. "It's Wilson, let me in!"

Eric and Sarah shook themselves free and both went to the door. Craig Wilson came in wide-eyed and sat down. He noticed they both looked a little rumpled but said nothing. "I just got off my shift and thought you should know a new development."

"Go ahead," said Eric.

"A roughneck from the oil rig on your property came to the precinct to report that someone else is missing."

106

Eric became very somber and said, "In Arkwell Oil speak, that means 'crossed-off the list'."

"What?" asked Wilson.

Eric explained the connections between the missing persons list and the mattress notes in Bodien's apartment.

"I can't believe it!" said Wilson.

Eric suggested an APB for the missing person but feared the outcome. With the first assassin and Bodien dead, there had to be another shooter. That might be whoever had tried to kill Eric in the parking lot.

The three sat in stunned silence. What did "cross-offs" mean? What did those workers know that made them marked men?

"I think a visit to the oil rig is in order," Eric said. "Maybe somebody can give me a clue about this missing person."

"That should be my job," Wilson said. "After all, Eric, somebody wants you dead!"

Eric feared any guilty parties might clam up if an officer asked questions. Besides, Wilson's captain had ordered him off the case. Wilson reluctantly agreed but said he would be available whenever Eric called.

A few minutes after Wilson left, Eric said, "Sarah, I must get to the bottom of this mess. How many more innocent people are going to die?" He kissed Sarah good night, and they squeezed hands.

Eric drove to the operating rig to talk with the roughnecks on night shift. Any clue might help.

Chapter 17

As Eric drove to the oil rig, it busily churned through clay, sand and limestone. He recognized everyone on the night shift except the man who had replaced the missing person. Eric found Joseph and asked how things were going. "Not good, Mr. Bonfield. I can't talk here. I'll text you later for a meeting."

Eric walked over to other men on break. None of them knew anything about the missing roughneck. Eric returned to his office and waited for Joseph's text.

Joseph would meet Eric in the parking lot of his office about midnight. Eric didn't care much for parking lots these days, especially at midnight, but it would have to do.

The hours dragged by as Eric waited. He caught up on Megan's pile of consulting work. At 12:00, he stepped into the darkness and onto the parking lot pavement still hot from the Arkansas summer sun. The humidity stifled his breathing. A movement in the bushes indicated that Joseph had arrived. Eric moved out of the direct beam of a weak parking lot lamp to meet Joseph.

Joseph began. "Mr. Bonfield, something very bad is going on. Our workers disappear, one after the other. Since I started working on the rig several people have gone missing, and new roughnecks take their place. I've worked oil fields for years but never have I seen turnover like this."

"Any ideas what's happening? Did the men who disappeared say anything before they went missing?"

"I see a pattern. After they work on a drill rig, a foreman sends them to already drilled producing wells; then they disappear. I remember one roughneck wandered back to our rig. As he shook his head, he said, 'This is weird. Something is being pumped down that well that doesn't look right.' The next day he didn't come to work."

Eric said, "You may have found the reason for their disappearance. Good work, Joseph."

Joseph said, "Thanks, but I have to go." As he turned, Eric heard the crack of a rifle, and Joseph slumped to the ground. Eric ducked. A second round passed harmlessly overhead and hit a No Parking sign. Eric knelt by Joseph and looked for the wound. Fortunately for Joseph, turning saved his life. The bullet grazed his skull, which bled, but it wasn't a mortal wound. Eric's rental car shielded them from the shooter. He drew his Glock, quickly held his gun over the car hood, and chanced a random shot in the general direction of the rifle. Eric heard crashing in the brush as the would-be assassin apparently fled.

"I'll get you to a hospital," said Eric.

Joseph groaned, "My head hurts so bad!"

Eric helped Joseph into his car and drove to the nearest ER. In the hospital, Eric prayed that God would restore Joseph's health. Joseph struck Eric as a good man with a high moral sense. He had taken a risk to tell Eric what he had seen and heard. The ER doctor assured Eric that his friend would have a headache and a sensitive area on the side of his skull, but full recovery could be expected.

"Thank God!"

Police arrived to take their testimony. Eric left the hospital and went to his apartment to try to get some sleep. Events seemed to be unfolding.

An e-mail from the hospital greeted Eric when he awakened: Joseph was doing fine. Eric said a prayer of thanksgiving and got ready for the day. Since the assassin seemed to preferred nighttime, Eric felt less cautious during the day and took the most direct route to the hospital.

"Hey, Joseph, How are you feeling?"

Joseph sat up in bed. "Food's not bad," he said with a forced smile as he swallowed toast and eggs. "I am doing well, it seems. The staff here are very good to me. They say I can leave today. If my wife was home, she would take care of me. But she is in California visiting relatives. She does not need to come home since I only have a headache."

"Excellent! I know you were targeted by Arkwell Oil, so what I'm about to say may seem crazy, but hear me out. I have a proposal. I need a partner to work as an undercover agent to discover what Arkwell Oil is all about and why so many workers disappear. Interested?"

Joseph smiled and thought a moment. "I think I would like that. This whole situation is crazy. Something needs to be done."

"You must understand that this is potentially a very dangerous project. I will have your back throughout the time you would do this, but there are no absolute guarantees of safety. I just don't know how else to find out what is going on with the missing workers."

"When do I start?" Joseph's smile broadened.

Eric nodded his head and smiled back. "Here's the plan I'm thinking about . . ." He had formulated the idea while driving to the hospital!

"Sounds interesting, Dr. Bonfield . . . ."

"Wait a minute, Joseph. My name is Eric. Please call me that."

"All right, Eric. It is just that in my culture someone of your authority is treated with respect, which means using a title."

"Not a problem when we're in a place where certain people can hear and wonder about our connection. But when it's you and me, it's Eric; clear?"

"I got it, Eric."

Maybe Joseph can help pry open the door of Arkwell Oil. Joseph agreed to rest at home for a day while his head healed. Then, unannounced, he would report back to work. The rest of the plan depended on reactions of other players in this theater of the oil rig. Of course, there must be an alternate plan if this one did not turn out well. And, if an alternate plan failed . . . he had better be prepared to think fast! Eric's training as a geologist required him to develop alternate approaches if the first one failed. He liked to apply the scientific method in all areas of his life, except . . . maybe when it came to Sarah and God! He smiled to himself.

Back at the office, Eric contacted Sheriff Hanson and an FBI friend to let them know what he was planning. They reluctantly agreed to stay in the background until Eric called for help. They had learned that Eric usually did things for good reasons.

He found the expected stack of work Megan had placed on his desk for that day. He thanked his efficient office manager and dove into the pile. A couple hours later he came up for air. Megan stuffed envelopes, typed reports, and responded to phone and e-mail messages as he cranked out responses to his clients. Eric felt relieved that these patient people stuck with him. None of them had jumped ship during his absences.

Then his eyes fell on a different sort of request. Someone in the county, not far from Sarah's farm, complained about well water quality. It was a cryptic message, "My cattle gittin' sick." Eric's brain kicked into high gear. He immediately called Nick Wendel, the farmer. "Never seen nothin' like it," Nick told Eric. "I been runnin' cows on this place fer 20 years. Always had good water and hay. But the last few weeks they been turnin' sickly. I brung out the vet and he said the water must be bad. Reckon you could look at it?"

"Yes, I can. I'll come out this afternoon if that's all right with you?"

"Sooner the better!"

"Right. Be there in an hour." Eric sat back in his chair and mumbled something.

"What did you say," asked Megan, looking up.

"Oh, just connecting dots, that's all."

Eric gathered collection bottles, an ice chest, and various gear to sample Nick Wendel's well water. Then he stopped by a local grocery store for ice. He always collected water specimens according to protocol. Samples must be kept cool and well-sealed so all chemical species can be measured. On the way to the farm, Eric wondered if there was a link to water under Sarah's farm and Wendel's wells. This might or might not be related to

Arkwell Oil's activities, but Eric had suspicions. He knew that things are not always totally straightforward when it comes to the movement of groundwater through rocks and soils.

Nick greeted Eric and showed him some of the ill cattle. Two deceased cows awaited the dead animal truck. For Nick, this was a disaster. Small operation farmers live close to the edge, and a setback like this could mean a lean year of income. Nick took Eric to his main well. Eric asked if Nick remembered how deep the well might be.

"Near as I can recollect, it's about 350 feet down to water."

Puzzled, Eric thought the Arkwell wells should be much deeper than that. But if that operation is as sleazy as everything else, leaks in their well casings might happen at any depth. Eric took several samples of water and quickly iced them in his cooler.

"What about water in your house, Nick, any problems there?"

"None I know of. 'Course, we always take our house water from a county water line that runs by our place. Hope I don't have to start usin' that water fer cows. That stuff is terrible expensive."

"Nick, depending on what I discover from the analysis of this well water, you just might have to start doing that very thing until the problem can be solved . . . if it can be solved."

Eric did not want to promise Nick much. A contaminated aquifer might take years to clean up.

Nick said, "Appreciate you comin' out right quick."

"I'll put this analysis on a fast track." Eric hurried off.

On his way back to town Eric took the water samples to a local environmental company for analysis. A lab technician promised results by the next day. Eric returned to his office just as Megan was leaving. She had accumulated more work for him to do. As she left, she called over her shoulder, "See you Sunday in church, Eric. In case you forgot, this is Friday."

"Right! Thanks for the reminder." Eric often lost all sense of what day it was when he became absorbed in a case. Her comment meant that Megan would not be in to work Saturday when the environmental lab sent their results. So, he needed to be around to print out the e-mail attachment as soon as it arrived. He could see the results on his cell phone but needed a hard copy for Nick Wendel.

Although it was late, Eric wasn't ready to leave work just yet. He wanted to understand the geology under Sarah and Nick's properties. Arkwell Oil had not released any well logs describing strata their bits penetrated. Instead, Eric used logs provided by water well drillers and a few wildcat oil wells drilled some distance away. Such work proved painstaking and tedious. Drillers' water well logs do not meet the same standards of oil company well logs. This required Eric to do lots of guessing in the absence of hard data. After exhausting all resources, Eric yawned and stretched. The geological story was beginning to unfold.

Eric looked at his watch. Seven o'clock. *I am starving!* He punched in Sarah's number. "Sarah, I know it's late, but would you like to join a hungry bear for dinner?"

Sarah giggled. "As long as I'm not what's for dinner!"

"Don't tempt me," he said with a sly chuckle.

"It so happens you caught me working late at the law office. I haven't eaten either."

"Great!" Eric said. "Let's go to Antonio's, if you're up for Italian."

"As long as it's with you, that's all I ask," she purred.

Eric's heart jumped a beat. "I'll meet you there in twenty minutes. See you." Closing the connection, he mused that Sarah's voice did something to him unlike any other.

On the drive to Antonio's, Eric thought about his relationship with Sarah. She had hired him to do an investigation. *And so I am investigating.* By default, he also was sort of her body guard. *Well, not really a body guard, but I look out for her well-being.* Sarah had no family and appeared lonely. *What about her friends?* Most lived in Little Rock, and they didn't visit much. *How about Jean as a friend?* He shook his head and thought, *With friends like Jean . . . .*

Eric wasn't clear about the way Sarah came on to him. *Was that just her nature?* He knew she was a first-born child, and he knew about differences in the birth order of siblings. Eric himself was the middle of three brothers. *Is that why I think the way I do?*

He didn't know how he should react to Sarah. It wasn't that he resisted her overtures. He smiled. No. Sarah appealed to him in many ways. They had similar church backgrounds and seemed compatible that way. They were both clear thinkers. Eric enjoyed her company, and he appreciated her beauty. Sarah wouldn't appear in Miss Arkansas contests. *But how important is a super model if I am looking for . . . .* Eric paused in thought. *Who am I looking for?*

Up to now, Eric had resigned himself to the life of a bachelor. He enjoyed his lifestyle; he earned a decent income. He liked where he lived, and the varied work kept his days interesting. Occasionally he dated, but nothing serious ever developed. His family lived not too far away, and he visited them occasionally. *Am I really looking for a . . .* he had a hard time even thinking the word . . . *wife?*

He and Sarah had enjoyed a few romantic moments. At least the other evening's embrace on the sofa didn't count as client and consultant talking business! *Get yourself together, Eric. Analyze this situation like you would a geology or crime problem; think clearly.*

Then Eric caught himself saying out loud, "This is ridiculous! Do I treat romance like a water drainage problem? That is dumb!"

How true; he could do geology or private investigative work using scientific methods, but would that work in matters of the heart? Eric sighed. Perhaps he was taking all this too seriously. Sarah might be reaching out because of stressful situations facing her right now. After the case passed into history and things settled down, everything might cool off. Sarah and he might return to the way they were before they met.

Then another thought crossed his mind. *Can life ever return to exactly the way it was after a traumatic event?* If he thought about it honestly, the answer screamed loudly. *Everything changes. Everything? Well, almost!*

And what does God think about all this? He paused and offered a prayer for guidance. He really needed it! Eric drove the rest of the way to the restaurant wishing for . . . he really wasn't sure for what.

Eric parked the rental car and ran into the restaurant. Sarah was waiting for him in a chair by the door. When she saw him, she jumped up and ran to him. Smiling, she gave him a hug. An evening out with Eric made her heart beat faster and her eyes sparkle. She felt safe and secure standing beside this tall, handsome man. His calm, assuring manner comforted her. It seemed that her world could fall apart, and maybe it already had, but Eric would be there to help her put the pieces back together, at least in some way.

They ordered dinner and engaged in casual conversation. Then Eric quietly described what Joseph had told him about disappearing workers. He summarized the near-tragic shooting incident, Joseph's hospitalization, and his pending recovery. Then he unfolded his plan to take Joseph alongside to unravel the web surrounding Arkwell Oil Company.

Sarah sat spellbound. *Was this real life?* It sounded more like action in a novel or movie. "But won't that be dangerous for Joseph? What if they decide to kill him?"

"I've warned Joseph. But he wants to help. He'll wear a tiny cell phone and a well-hidden locater unit to help me keep track of him at all times. I'm going to be on twenty-four hour watch. Plus, he will be wearing a Kevlar vest to provide some protection from bullets."

"You think of everything," Sarah said admiringly. Then rather sheepishly she said, "I mean you are a great planner."

Eric took the compliment with humility. Whatever planning skills he possessed, he attributed to his genetic makeup and parental upbringing. His father and mother had trusted him with responsibilities beyond his years. He owed them a lot. Later, his training as a scientist had honed his innate abilities. Planning is key to any successful completion of a project, and Eric usually took the time to plan well.

Dinner went by smoothly as they talked and made eyes at each other, or did Sarah make eyes and Eric respond? Either way, eye romance prevailed. Eventually they finished dinner, and he escorted Sarah to her car.

"Do you have time to come home and let me fix coffee?" she asked. "I baked a special pie just for you."

Eric agreed without fanfare but with hidden eagerness. *What a delight to be with her!* Sarah's joyous spirit and attractive smile made him want to hold her close and never let her go. He drove behind Sarah's car to her farm. Although they arrived long after night had fallen, Eric remembered the attractive landscaping around the house. Sarah's organizing skills showed in everything she touched.

The blackberry pie was the *piece de resistance* of the evening. As they ate, they talked about trivial things. Afterwards, they moved to the couch in the living room.

Sarah was the first to speak. "Eric, I hope you don't think me too bold, but I have to say that I am taken with you! You are such a wonderful person. You . . . you . . . ," Sarah said as she reached for his hands.

Eric took her hands in his, "Sarah, I have never met any woman like you. You are brave, thoughtful, kind, and a person of faith. I know you hired me to do an investigation. But what I feel right now is something far different than solving a case. I feel about you as I have never before felt about anyone."

Sarah's eyes glistened. "Nor have I felt this way toward anyone before." Then she blushed a brilliant red. A long pause followed as they stared deeply into each other's eyes, trying to read any messages encoded there.

Finally Eric murmured, "Sarah, I don't really know what love is supposed to be like between a woman and a man. I am ignorant of these things. But, after all this is over, that is the investigation, I want us to think about what we mean to each other. Do you understand what I'm saying?"

Sarah could hardly contain herself, "You said the most beautiful word in our language, Eric. You used the word *love*. As best I know now, I feel as you do."

There followed another long moment of eye analysis. Then they moved until his arms were around her waist and her arms around his neck. They drew closer still until their eyes closed and their lips joined as one. At last their lips parted and their eyes opened. Each stared deeply into the soul of the other.

Eric felt his breath barely coming and going. He did not want this moment to end. *But I know this can't last forever.* As they separated slightly, he said, "Sarah, can we make an agreement. Let's try to let our passions cool a little. There are many difficult days ahead in this investigation. I don't think we want to be distracted, or it could be lethal, and I mean that literally." His face was grave, although his eyes revealed excitement.

Sarah nodded her head grudgingly. Her mind knew what he said was true. Her heart spoke a different language, but she must let her head rule for now. They rose from this special place of awareness, holding hands and never losing eye contact. Eric gently kissed her on the lips and wordlessly moved toward the door.

Sarah watched as he drove away. All she could think about was that he had used the word "love". Saying the word made her whole body tingle. She knew he had spoken from his heart and his mind. Funny, she thought, *we both expressed emotion and logic, those two sides of life which don't always have the same points of view!* She went to the kitchen and began to wash dishes. She wondered if this would be a forecast of things to come. *Will we share our lives through the simple acts of eating together and talking?*

On the way back to his apartment, Eric thought of something else and rang Sarah. "Would you like to go with me to church on Sunday?" Her answer was enthusiastic. *Good. This relationship, if it persists, must always be on a higher plain than just feelings.* His religious life meant much to him. His parents, both Christians, had taken him to church shortly after he was born. He was baptized as an infant, and he grew up learning the lessons of Sunday school and church. He became a believer early in life.

Faith was a powerful force in Eric's life. Unlike many of his high school friends, Eric's academics and his faith background merged fairly easily.

Some of his acquaintances had renounced their faith when they attended the university. Others struggled to merge what they studied in school with teachings of the church. Eric, on the other hand, saw all of life as a whole. He felt his academic work must somehow be consistent with his faith in God. If an issue seemed to be in conflict, he spent time working through various ways for both views to be consistent. Eric read widely and enjoyed lively discussions about science and faith. To him it was an exercise in building a better world-view.

Chapter 18

*S*aturday dawned with blustery wind and rain. *A miserable day to work on the rigs. I hope Joseph is well enough to go back to work next week.* The results of Nick's well water analysis were expected this morning. Eric was trying to connect the death of Danny Isaacs with the killing of Bodien Kessel and Nick Wendel's water well problem. Somehow, Arkwell's "oil" wells must tie them together.

Finally the lab director called to tell Eric the results of his analysis. "You can read the data," he said, "but I have to ask where you got those samples, if you don't mind telling me. That stuff is positively lethal!"

"That's what I feared. They come from a farmer's stock well."

"Whoa! I'd plug that well immediately!"

Eric rang off and dashed to his computer to run the report. It didn't take a minute for Eric to agree with the lab director. Then Eric phoned Nick Wendel. "Nick, this is Eric Bonfield. The water in your stock well is dangerous. No wonder cattle are dying. Please plug the well immediately and switch to county water so your cattle can drink safely."

Nick said, "Not happy to hear that, but got to keep them cows alive!"

After Eric hung up, his mind whirled. *How widespread is this problem? Had other farmers in the area experienced similar issues?* He examined a plat map of the area that showed the locations and owners of farms around Sarah's property. He jotted down the names of the owners. Then he began making calls.

After a lengthy series of phone conversations, Eric leaned back in his chair. It squeaked, reminding him again to ask Megan to order a new one. Just as he suspected, farm wells south of Sarah's "oil field" (a misnomer, he thought) had sick cows. Those wells north, east, and west did not have problems. Eric knew the strata under the land in this part of Arkansas tilted downward to the south. This meant that gravity would naturally pull the groundwater in that direction.

According to the environmental lab's report, Nick's well had enormously high concentrations of harmful byproducts from industrial chemical plants. The analysis contained no petroleum products used in drilling. This meant that the contamination was not the result of accidental leaking from a well but was intentionally inserted into the groundwater.

Eric shook his head as he thought about the disposal of leftovers from manufacturing processes. Such residues should be recycled, destroyed, or disposed of in some environmentally-friendly way. Recycling is typically expensive. Destruction and disposal are also expensive. Burial in a specially constructed landfill is not cheap.

Eric feared that Arkwell Oil was using a fourth alternative by illegally dumping waste without consideration of the consequences. It looked as if contaminated wells were the result on Nick's farm and other farms south of Sarah's place.

The only thing required for illegal dumping is a tanker to pick up waste, then haul it to a non-approved site, dump it, and return for more. Cheap, efficient, and who would know, except maybe some farmers with sick cows or people who end up in the hospital or morgue.

Eric knew that to stop this illegal dumping someone must identify the existence of a dump site and report it to state authorities. That sounds easy, but proof must be clear and unambiguous. Sick cows will not trigger a full scale assault on the perpetrator.

Only extensive analytical evidence could serve as proof of the nasty liquids source, and Eric had already started that. He didn't think it would be too difficult to map the point of contamination once he entered well data into a GIS. But intermediate agencies could get in the way of an investigation. Arkwell Oil seemed to be cozy with a certain police captain who never investigated problems with that company.

State agencies usually have jurisdiction and could bypass local authorities who might be bought off. However, before he contacted the state, Eric needed to be certain the sick cows were not some fluke but a pattern traceable directly to Arkwell wells. Fortunately, most of the farmers had discontinued using their contaminated water sources.

He turned to his computer and did a statistical analysis of any reports of illness or death among farm animals in areas where Arkwell Oil had drilled wells since their first operation in Arkansas. It did not take long to find a probable connection. Illness or sudden death of animals, and in a few cases, humans, occurred shortly after Arkwell began drilling wells nearby. Eric snapped his fingers and smiled grimly, "Gotcha!"

Proximity is easy to prove. But coincidence can rule in court cases. Eric then searched for sources of industrial waste products. Large chemical manufacturing plants popped up and, surprise, surprise, their locations lay no more than a short drive from Arkwell's apparently fake oil wells. "Looks like an open and shut case," Eric said to no one in particular. But he knew simple connections are not so obvious in the courtroom. Cause and effect must be conclusively connected.

Dumping is one thing. Contamination and destruction of life forms is another. Both must be proved in order to shut down the operations completely and begin the arduous task of water cleanup, which would be no easy matter. Any company responsible for such a groundwater disaster would probably go belly-up due to inability to pay for the cleanup. This would leave the government with most of the tab. Taxpayers are usually the final source of funds in most cases like this. *That just isn't fair.* He wished for a better system that prevented such things from happening, but nothing else showed on the horizon.

Then there was the matter of the missing roughnecks and at least two murders that somehow were connected to the contaminated groundwater.

Who would testify against responsible parties? Eric might gather enough evidence to close down Arkwell Oil. The polluting would stop and Arkwell Oil might dissolve into history. But those responsible for the missing persons and deaths might go free. Lack of evidence connecting Arkwell personnel to the apparent murders meant killers might escape with losing only their company but not their personal freedoms or their lives.

Since Eric found himself in the middle of this mess, he felt responsible to gather evidence to prove the full extent of Arkwell Oil's criminality. *Talk about heavy lifting!* Eric sighed. His work had hardly begun. He scratched his head and desperately prayed that Joseph could discover the truth about Arkwell's missing workers. Even with miserable weather, Saturday had yielded some answers. Later that day Eric called Joseph. "How are you doing?"

"I am doing well. I plan to return to the rig Monday night during my regular shift. It will be interesting to see the looks on faces when I come back!"

Eric agreed. He especially wanted to know who reacted and how. The day concluded with a light rain. When Eric left for home, no bullets greeted him. *Very nice!* This he thought with a touch of sarcasm. Takeout oriental would have to suffice for a late dinner. All other fast food places had closed for the night. He suddenly felt exhausted and wished only for his bed.

Eric's alarm woke him, with a reminder that Sunday is meant to be a day of rest. He really needed it! He picked up Sarah, and they drove to his church. The service encouraged them both. Eric sensed a bit of pride sitting next to his pretty client, dressed in a becoming white outfit. Eric's friends greeted him and Sarah at the close of service; their curiosity got the best of them. Eric usually sat alone or with other men, so what's with the youthful beauty who came to church with him? Eric did not satisfy their curiosity but used his courtroom experience involving environmental problems to deflect their unspoken questions.

After church, they had dinner at a local restaurant and Eric caught Sarah up on what he knew about the case. He explained about contaminated water wells and sick cows. She was shocked with the news.

"Wow," she said. "You found what the company is doing! That is great investigative work." Then she slyly smiled and said, "I'm glad I hired you." They both laughed.

Afterwards Eric drove Sarah to her farm and lingered while she changed into comfortable jeans and shirt. They sat discretely in the living room, a cautious suitor and a willing hostess. She sat on the sofa. He occupied an easy chair. Sensing that they needed to relax, Sarah suggested a table game. Eric normally considered such things a waste of time, but they must do something to keep their hormones and hands in check. She found a somewhat challenging game, and they spent the next couple of hours in mild competition. Sarah let Eric win part of the time. She didn't want to discourage the novice.

A light supper was in order. As they ate, they talked about their backgrounds. Eric described his parents and their strong differences. His mother was soft-spoken, kind, and encouraging. In contrast, his father's austerity had discouraged the children from displaying or talking much about their feelings, except when Dad wasn't around. Not that he was unkind; he just didn't say much. Eric's parents lived only a couple of hours away. Would Sarah like to visit them sometime . . . oops . . . *wished I hadn't said that.*

She could have jumped at the chance but wisely suggested they wait until after the investigation. Eric mentally wiped his brow, relieved with her discretion. In their culture, to visit parents with a person of the opposite gender meant more than saying, "I want you to meet a friend." Quizzing and inspection for suitability as a spouse accompanied such visits. Eric did not want to expose Sarah to such scrutiny. They were not ready for such an examination. Meeting parents too early might be a faux pas of huge proportions.

Sarah talked about her mother, who had died so young, and of her father's tragic accident. Then she lapsed into memories of her brother, Danny, the young man whom Eric would never meet, but whose fall from an oil rig had turned Eric's life upside down, as well as Sarah's. Her family differed significantly from Eric's. Her mother and father both verbally expressed their love for one another and their children—something that Eric had rarely known from his dad.

"I haven't heard you talk about your siblings," Sarah asked. "You have some, don't you?"

"I'm the middle of three brothers. The eldest, Arnold, lives in Nashville and runs a large grocery store. He has a wife and one young son. Jacob is unmarried and loves the out-of-doors. He works for the New York State parks as a ranger."

"Sounds like males dominate your family. I wonder if that would influence the genders of your children." She paused and blushed the most beautiful red. Eric laughed, and this broke an awkward moment. They giggled like teenagers on a first date. Eric knew they both wanted to talk about marriage.

Finally Eric said, "Look, Sarah, we both know what's on each other's minds, so let's stop kidding ourselves. What are you looking for in a life partner?" He couldn't bring himself to say the "h" word.

Suddenly, Sarah turned serious and said, "Well, I must admit I've not thought about it very much. I've been focused on building a career and running a farm by myself. I guess those girlish dreams teenagers think about disappeared when life took on the seriousness of . . . ." She paused and tears began to form in her eyes.

Eric said, "I'm certain you have experienced a world of hurt. How hard it must be to lose both parents and your only sibling!"

His words allowed Sarah to gather her thoughts. She spoke haltingly of how painful parental death can be. And for her brother to die on her farm was almost too much. Eventually, Sarah regrouped and said, with a straight face, "I'm interested in someone with solid character who puts God first,

124

wants the best for others, creates a sense of stability and security, and . . ." she glanced shyly at Eric and added, "is six feet tall, has brown hair, blue eyes . . . ." Then she laughed out loud! "Sorry, I just couldn't pass that up!" They both laughed. "And what about you? Who is your complete woman?"

"Well," Eric began, "I've been around the block a few times but, as you've said, I don't know a lot about women. A family of all boys doesn't prepare one for this sort of thing. I want someone who is faithful, loving, spiritually alive, has a sense of family first, and . . . ." He looked straight at Sarah as he added, laughing, "Is about five feet, four inches tall, has brown hair and hazel eyes." Sarah joined in and when the laughter subsided, they stared at each other across the room, blue eyes meeting hazel eyes for a long minute.

Eric rose, came to her, and lifted Sarah gently by both hands until their breaths touched each other's faces. "Sounds to me like a match," he said, kissing her soundly. Sarah relaxed in his arms and felt a shiver all over. A magic 30 seconds followed.

Then Eric took charge of the moment, knowing they must go no further. "Sarah, I've got to leave. Business starts early tomorrow."

A second but not-so-prolonged kiss followed, and they parted. Sarah waved a flirting hand as he got into his car. He acknowledged it and smiled deeply.

As Eric drove to his apartment, a thunderbolt hit his brain. *Did I inadvertently propose to Sarah!* His eyes flew wide open and sweat popped on his forehead—that always happened when he felt stress. He barely knew the woman. *What was I thinking?* Then he felt slightly relieved when he remembered that they had agreed to wait until after the investigation to build their relationship. *It will be hard to wait!*

Sarah watched Eric drive away. When the tail lights of his car disappeared, she gave a great sigh. She had just experienced the most romantic moment of her life. Her mind filled with willowy thoughts. Words Eric had said floated back to her. *Had he really proposed?* Then she shook herself. *No, not at all. But he had spoken from his heart.* How wonderful it felt.

She collapsed onto her sofa and relived the previous moments, relishing each exchange of words. Tonight her dreams would be sweet, as would Eric's.

Back at his apartment, Eric called Joseph's cell phone, "Are you ready for Monday night?"

"No problem. I will drive my own car."

"And I will be at Sarah's house in case of trouble. Your tiny cell phone must be on all the time and set not to ring or vibrate should some random call come in. Are you still all right with this plan?"

"Of course, Eric. I want to see justice done. I will be listening to everything tomorrow night."

Eric smiled. *I picked the right man to help solve Danny's murder.* Joseph would do well—that is, if they both survived the next few days.

Chapter 19

Eric rose early Monday morning. The clear sky permitted the sun to beam through his apartment window. After a light breakfast, he went to his office to work until Joseph's early night shift began. Then he drove to Sarah's farm and parked behind her house to avoid being seen by trucks that rumbled onto the property. Eric listened on his phone as Joseph arrived at the company's makeshift parking area. Gravel crunched under Joseph's feet as he walked toward the noisy rig.

The first person Joseph met was one of the long-time workers. Eric heard the man gasp as if he'd seen a ghost. "Joseph! I thought . . . we were told . . . that you are dead!"

"Not quite, amigo! As you can see, I am fully here and human and not a ghost."

The other roughnecks crowded around Joseph. They shook his hand and asked about the bandage on his head. But the biggest surprise came from Murphy Edwards as he walked out of the mudlogger's shack. At first, Edwards was speechless. When he managed to compose himself, he said they had already replaced Joseph on this shift; he added that Joseph might take a late night shift if he wished. Edwards kept looking at Joseph's bandage and finally asked about it.

"Oh, it is nothing. Just a scratch. I'll take that other shift. Thanks."

Joseph walked to his car and drove away from the rig. Edwards immediately grabbed his cell phone and disappeared behind the shack.

After taking side roads to a café rendezvous, Joseph met Eric for debriefing. They took a table in the back where they could see whoever walked in. Eric wanted to hear Joseph's first-hand report, but he had guessed most of what happened from the hidden phone conversation. Edwards obviously had told everyone Joseph was dead, and he had immediately hired a replacement roughneck.

"How would Edwards know about me being shot and killed unless he was in on the deal?"

"It sure looks that way. Edwards is also the only Arkwell Oil rep I told about the cut harness. He might be the guy who hires thugs, but somebody higher up probably calls the plan for him. Who that person might be is anybody's guess."

They agreed that Joseph would return to the rig later that night on his adjusted work schedule.

"Joseph, if you sense trouble, I'll be waiting at Sarah's farm house to bail you out."

After their conversation, Joseph drove home to rest up for his new shift. Eric went to his apartment, also to sleep, as best he could, until his watch began.

Joseph smiled as he returned to the rig for his late night shift. *This could be interesting!* While he worked, Eric listened to conversations via Joseph's cell phone. The oil crew displayed their usual banter and jokes, but now and then a muffled conversation indicated that the roughnecks were puzzled. They had heard about Joseph and did not understand why Edwards had told them that Joseph was dead. Why had Edwards replaced him so quickly? Joseph let the men talk and ask questions. He listened and let the conversation drift as it would.

Edwards himself was not present during the shift that night. When the shift concluded, Joseph walked cautiously toward his car. Clouds had rolled in and no stars were out. Beyond lights illuminating the rig, it was pitch black. Out of sight of the other workers, Joseph called Eric and asked what he ought to do. He sensed danger.

"This is a very dangerous time," Eric cautioned. "Be alert for anything out of the ordinary. The Kevlar vest that I borrowed from the sheriff is designed to reduce your vulnerability to bullets. But the vest won't stop a sharpshooter who aims at your head."

Joseph kept his head down as he groped toward the car. Eric had told him what to look for. Nearing his vehicle, he scanned the darkness for any lights or reflections off a scope. He used his remote starter from a safe distance to see if a bomb had been planted in the car. When nothing happened, he got in and drove down the makeshift lane toward the county road that went by Sarah's farmhouse.

At the intersection of the lane and the county road, he maneuvered the vehicle in a manner Eric had suggested the day before: he suddenly jerked the wheel the opposite direction that a sniper might expect. The movement saved his life. A bullet nicked the front window support on the driver's side. Joseph gunned the motor and sped away.

From his listening post on Sarah's front porch, Eric had a clear view of the oil rig road where Joseph would exit. Using authority to shoot under extreme situations, he had borrowed equipment from a friend at the local Army National Guard. Eric accurately located the source of the shot. He trained a high-powered sniper rifle just to the left of the bullet's source and pulled the trigger five times, spraying the shooter's likely position.

In the nocturnal quietness, Eric heard a cry of pain. He dropped the rifle and ran toward the spot, Glock in hand. His ear detected thrashing in the bushes just ahead. The assassin appeared to be wounded. That made the situation dangerous for Eric. *How badly wounded is this guy?* As he neared the noise in the bushes, three bullets scarred the ground in his general direction.

Fortunately for Eric, the shots missed by several feet. He aimed again and squeezed off two rounds toward the source. Another groan came from the darkness and a weak voice cried out, "All right. Don't shoot."

Eric suspected a trap, so he didn't answer. He walked toward the shooter, his steps cautious as a cat. On a hunch, Eric tossed a rock 20 feet to his right. Another rifle blast. This time Eric could almost make out the figure. He squeezed off a round that clearly found its mark. A gasp and silence followed. Eric moved quickly to close the gap between him and the shooter. He played his flashlight over the person sprawled there by a bush. He could not have been more surprised.

Jean Myers lay on the ground, her blood flowing into the black soil. A rifle lay at her side. Eric cradled her head with his arm and felt for a pulse.

"You don't have to do that!" Jean exclaimed. "I ain't dead yet!"

Eric almost leaped backward. "How bad are you hurt?"

"You got me in the shoulder once and in the leg twice. Get me to a doc!"

Eric was too shocked to do anything but obey. His surprise stopped him from asking any questions. Jean's wounds didn't appear life-threatening, so he did a hasty bandage job, helped her up, and assisted her to his car. He put a sheet over the back seat and her rifle in his trunk. "This is a rental and I don't want blood all over it!" Jean just grunted.

As he drove to the closest ER, Eric called the police and hospital. Medical staff took her to surgery and removed two bullets lodged in her body. One rifle bullet had passed through her leg. Eric called Wilson and asked for a police guard at her room.

The next day Jean was alert. Eric accompanied a police officer during the interrogation. Wilson told Eric that this officer could he trusted, since he was not under the direct thumb of the suspicious Captain.

Eric stared at Jean Myers, the assassin. *Who is she?* During the session Jean waved her rights.

On probing who had hired her to do the shooting, she replied, "Ain't tellin' that. Would get myself killed for certain if I squealed. You all can understand that, right?"

Eric whispered to the officer, who nodded in agreement.

"Look, Jean, I understand your fear. But, Eric Bonfield here was the object of some of your bullets. He could testify against you when you are charged with attempted murder. Arkansas does not consider this a trivial crime. They won't inject you for this at Cummins, but if you can be linked to real murders, then things could get interesting."

This seemed to unnerve Jean and she became anxious and looked at Eric. "You'd do that to me?"

"What do you mean? You did this to yourself."

Jean looked forlorn. "I know'd this couldn't turn out good. Look, I didn't ever really kill no one!"

Almost an admission!

Eric whispered in the interrogator's ear, after which the officer said, "You tried to kill someone last night. What makes me think you haven't been doing this all along? Did you plug Bodien?"

Jean's jaw dropped. "How'd you know it was me?"

It had been a hunch, but Eric had hit the target. The officer asked, "So you have killed someone, then?"

"Well, Bodien wasn't much of a person. He was a jerk. He made my life miserable."

"Did you lie in wait for him like you did for Joseph, or was there a confrontation?"

Jean's tongue cut loose. "Bodien did dirty work for Arkwell Oil Company, and I was his alibi, if he needed one." She would vouch that he was with her every time someone disappeared.

So Bodien was implicated! Eric was ecstatic.

Jean continued her story. When Bodien was paid for his services, he'd come to her all excited. At this, Jean glared and complained that Bodien never shared his spoils with her, and she got tired of this. After Danny died on the rig, Jean told Bodien she would not cover for him again. He became very angry and waved his hunting knife at her. This so infuriated Jean that she picked up his sniper rifle and emptied it into his "sorry carcass."

"Why were you and Bodien on Sarah's farm that night?" the officer asked.

"He was goin' to see his boss at the rig, and I wanted to tag along." Immediately Eric guessed the boss was Edwards. "When we got near there, we started to argue. That's when he threatened me."

The officer asked, "So, did you take Bodien's place in the company?"

"Yes." She found Bodien's employer and told him she had just killed Bodien and that she wanted his job. The employer wasn't happy with hiring a woman, but he gave her the job of bumping off Joseph and Eric.

The officer said, "I think there might be a possibility that the state would let you off with some sort of manslaughter charge for killing Bodien; they could call it self-defense. But those shots you took at Joseph and Eric carry attempted murder charges. Together this could mean a long time in prison. I know you are afraid of your boss, but you never know if you might get some leniency if you reveal who he is. I couldn't promise a thing. Just saying."

Jean mulled this over. "I got to think on that." And she was through talking.

Eric thanked the officer for letting him in on the interrogation and left the hospital. He tried to wrap his mind around Jean's story. She had done a good job of lying to him prior to tonight; he kicked himself for being taken in by her plausible stories. He usually could sense when people lied, but Jean had fooled him on the key points. He wondered, though, if the current story was completely true. Jean was an effective liar.

Jean knew Bodien had worked for someone in Arkwell Oil. Would she testify against the person she feared? This part of the case now resided in the hands of the law; Eric would serve only as a witness. If Jean refused to talk, the investigation might hit another wall. She could be tried for attempted murder and possible manslaughter. But that would be it! Nothing remained to stop other shooters on Arkwell's payroll from killing Joseph or anybody else, for that matter. If Joseph's undercover work continued, the danger might ratchet up.

After the interrogation, Eric and Joseph talked at length. Joseph wanted to return to work on the rig. He would pretend that nothing unusual had happened. He was concerned that the dent in his car might give rise to unwanted questions, and he wanted it repaired. Eric said he would foot the bill.

Eric decided he must catch Sarah up on the latest developments. He called her that morning. She was aghast. Shaking her head, she said, "I just can't believe Jean would do such a thing. Poor Joseph being shot at! And you in a shootout with Jean!"

"Maybe you can help me with a question I have about Jean. She seemed very comfortable using a sniper rifle. Where did she learn how to shoot?"

"Oh, I forgot to tell you much about Jean's background. She came from a family without a mother. Her mom left when Jean was only five, so her dad raised her. He was a hunter and took Jean along on his hunting trips. She was quite interested in guns and joined the high school gun club. They practiced with all sorts of weapons, including sniper rifles. She was really good. In fact, as a senior, she was second in the state shooting contest. I'm sorry I didn't tell you this earlier, but it never occurred to me that this was important."

"That makes a lot of sense, now. She just barely missed Joseph in a moving car. He is alive only because I told him how to turn onto the main road."

"I'm so glad she missed him!" Sarah said.

"Jean completely fooled me. Now I don't know if other people I've interviewed are telling the truth either."

Sarah shared Eric's uncertainty. They closed their conversation with a promise to pray for Joseph's safety.

Arriving late at his office in the morning, Eric started to tackle the work Megan had laid out for him. Then he turned and asked, "Megan, how did you know John was the one for you?"

Megan smiled and turned from her computer to face Eric. She knew such a question did not come out of the blue. "Well, Eric, I took my time and so did John. We dated for several months before we started to talk about life together. I had dated quite a bit and formed a mental image of the man I wanted to marry. It turns out John had done about the same. Once we put those ideas together it became obvious we would marry."

"That's amazing. But didn't you have lots of questions and feelings to work through?"

"Oh, sure. I think John decided we were right for each other before I did. My habit of orderliness took over. I wanted us to be certain. That's why we went to our pastor for premarital counseling. What an eye-opener that was! Lots of things came out that we would never have talked over or even thought about without that experience. After several sessions, I became convinced John would be my guy. He already knew I was his gal! That's the story!" She smiled again, her brown eyes glistening, as she returned to her work.

Eric stared into space. He realized that Megan had just given him a free counseling session right there in his own office. He knew he wanted a relationship like Megan and John displayed. Here were two level-headed people fully in love. They did thoughtful things for each other. John treated her with respect, and she committed herself to him like no one Eric had ever known. Megan's advice was gold, and it was free! "Thank you, Megan. You are a big help in more ways than one."

Megan kept her face turned toward the computer screen to hide her grin. "You are welcome. Now get back to work!"

Thinking about Megan's fresh insight, Eric thought about his relationship with Sarah. Megan was right about not rushing things. *Got to cool it down.*

After wiping off her smile, Megan turned back to Eric. "Oh, by the way, you may want to check out Mrs. Flynn's sinkhole problem. That situation is teetering on the brink of disaster; she is afraid her driveway might disappear overnight!"

"You are right! I'll get right on it." But he immediately forgot about sinkholes. Eric was thinking about Megan's advice on how to evaluate a relationship. Megan shook her head and smiled impishly. *Eric is so easily distracted.*

Chapter 20

*J*oseph's next shift back seemed routine. But Eric worried about routines, since monotony can take the place of caution. And that could lead to lethal consequences.

At the conclusion of Joseph's shift, one of the roughnecks took Joseph aside and spoke with caution. "Joseph, I don't know what's goin' on but I smell a rat. This outfit loses way too many workers. They disappear without a trace, and nobody comes by to check things out. The workers are just gone. What is up?"

Joseph answered with the skill of a wise communicator. "Amigo, I wonder what you think?"

"Seems to me the most dangerous place to be around here is workin' on the finished wells," the roughneck replied. "That's not the way it's supposed to be, Joseph! It's like the completed wells are jinxed. Somethin' goes on over there that ain't right."

"You may be onto something, my friend. Perhaps you are right. I would keep my head down if I were you".

"Thanks, I will." And the conversation ended.

Eric had listened to the discussion via Joseph's open cell phone. He asked Joseph to alert him when the worried worker finished his shift. "I think I should tail him, Joseph. He could be the next target."

After the shift change, the worker headed home, driving away from the rig and onto the county road that led into town. Eric followed at a discrete distance. Years of practice had honed his skills as a tail. He knew how to hold back just enough to avoid being seen. Half way to town, what Eric had feared happened.

Eric heard a report of gunfire, and he saw the worker's pickup swerve wildly. Eric could see where the shot came from, and he gunned his rental car onto the grassy area where the shooter was lurking. Bushes only partially hid the assassin, and the man with the weapon froze as he stared into Eric's headlights. That sealed his fate. Eric's car struck the man, knocking him over and sending his rifle flying. Eric braked to a stop and jumped out. He held his Glock on the shooter, who groaned and clutched his knee where the left fender hit him.

"All right," Eric shouted. "Who do you work for?" He hoped the shock of the moment might loosen the shooter's tongue.

"Edwards . . . Murphy Edwards."

That was exactly what Eric wanted to hear. "That name just might save you from a really long prison sentence," Eric said grimly. He called for help. A sheriff's deputy and an ambulance soon arrived. The criminal was taken to the nearest ER, then transferred to a hospital room, where he was kept under heavy guard. Eric filed charges at the sheriff's office so the man could be jailed for attempted murder as soon as he might leave the hospital.

The assassin's target had sustained no injuries. The roughneck had seen Eric's action and returned to the scene. He shook his head and declared, "I'm quittin' and movin' to Texas. I want no more of Arkwell Oil."

Eric guessed that bagging two hit men . . . or . . . women in such short order must be unnerving to Edwards and company higher-ups. Good. Maybe they would crack and do something to incriminate themselves even before charges could be brought.

No such luck. In fact, things took a turn for the worse. Desperate people do desperate things. That morning Eric arrived at his office and found Megan extremely agitated. "What's wrong?" he asked, recognizing danger. With a quivering finger, Megan pointed to the answering machine.

Eric listened with horror. A muffled voice spoke ominously, "If you want to see your 'client' alive again, get off this case now!"

136

"Oh, no! They've taken Sarah!" He slumped into his office chair and stared at the answering machine in disbelief.

Megan put a hand on his shoulder. "Eric, I don't know what's going on, but this is really serious. Are the police on the case?"

Eric gave a huge sigh and looked at Megan wearily. "I'm up against a powerful force with tentacles even into local law enforcement. I'm afraid to give this problem to the police. These criminals might do something to Sarah. The sheriff's office is the only local agency I have confidence in right now, and the only police officer I trust fully is Craig Wilson."

Megan withdrew her hand and scanned Eric's face. She understood his non-verbal language, and knew Eric would not give up. She also knew he needed time to decide what to do next. "Eric, I know you will do the right thing. That is built into you. I've never known anyone with such a strong moral sense. That's why I like working for you. You are a real Christian man."

Megan's affirmation brought a weak smile from Eric. He thanked her and stared for another moment at the answering machine. Then he got up and called Joseph. Megan heard Eric ask Joseph to pray for Sarah's safety and said they needed to meet in a couple of hours to talk strategy.

Just to be certain that this wasn't a crank call, Eric punched in Sarah's number. There was no pickup. He frowned and ended the call. Then Eric called an FBI friend and notified her about this kidnapping threat. He asked her to wait until he had time to sort things out. No use provoking the enemy to do something drastic.

Megan wasn't surprised when Eric turned to his desk, picked up a stack of papers, and sat down to write geological consulting reports. She knew that when Eric wanted his internal processing system to work on a difficult problem, he did routine tasks. By focusing on a completely different project, his subconscious could free itself to discover how to deal with an issue. He had picked up this habit from his father. Eric remembered how his dad, when faced with a problem, would disappear for a few hours; then he would return to the house ready to tackle the issue head on. Temporary isolation or distraction had freed his mind to deal with whatever faced him.

Although devastated at the news of Sarah, Eric threw himself into his work. In less than two hours of concentrated effort, he knocked out the reports. He slumped back in his chair, listened to its abrasive noise, and allowed himself to focus on the apparent kidnapping of Sarah.

How serious was this kidnapping? How real was the threat on her life? Was she being held against her will at some remote location or at her home? How desperate were these people? Or did they just use scare tactics? After all, Eric himself used scare methods to dislodge information from criminals. Now he had received his own medicine! He stroked his chin. *So this is how it feels!*

Eric bleakly stared at the floor. Not long ago he had worried about Sarah as a life partner. Then he and Megan had a conversation which brought common sense into the picture. Now he was worried about Sarah, but for a different reason. Her captors were playing on his emotions by threatening her life. How quickly things turn around! He faced the possible loss of someone he cared about.

Knowing he must move from feeling fear to thinking rationally, Eric thought about how to approach this new problem. Raw emotion had to give way to fresh ideas. *Life is a series of switches from emotion to reason, from reason to emotion, and back again.* He consciously released his mind from its bondage to panic, so he could find a creative solution.

For Eric, fresh ideas began with a moment of partial inspiration, a brief spark in his brain. Then, as the spark sputtered and slowly ignited, additional thoughts confirmed that the idea might be a keeper. He learned early in life to grab pencil and paper to write down the essence of an idea as soon as he thought of it. Otherwise, the thought might be lost.

After several minutes, Eric began sketching the kernel of a plan— enough to begin a discussion with Joseph. He looked at his watch. "Better get going," he said to Megan. "I told Joseph I'd meet him in two hours, and he will be waiting." Driving to a small café where he and Joseph would work out their strategy, Eric thanked God for Joseph. The chemistry between them generated energy and, he hoped, results.

Sure enough, Joseph's car was already in the parking lot. Eric rushed inside to find Joseph staking out a spot at the end of the room. Here they could talk without interruption, and anyone who came in the door could not escape their gaze. Considering the dangers they each experienced, keeping their eyes open for questionable visitors was essential.

Huddled in their booth and scribbling notes, they paused from time to time to allow their brains to cool and recharge. Coffee helped, and the waiter kept their cups full. They formed a tentative plan. If it didn't work, at least it wouldn't put Sarah in any more danger.

Joseph spoke quietly, "I will return to the oil rig and keep my eyes and ears open for anything that might give a clue about Sarah. Who knows? Maybe a loose tongue will spill something about where she is."

Eric said, "I don't like it, but I'll stay in town and wait at my office. They may be watching to see what I do next. If you discover anything, Joseph, I'll be ready to try and free Sarah. The rig is our source of information. And if anyone can find it, you can." Their conversation ended and the waiter beamed at the cash left on their table.

Returning to his office, Eric was on pins and needles; he paced back and forth. Megan told him to go see a client to get his mind off dead center.

"That's a good idea, Megan! Thanks." He headed for his car. "Rental cars," he mumbled. "I wish I had my pickup." But he knew days remained before its repair would be complete. He reached for the ignition and then realized something: he had locked the car that morning, but he now opened the door without unlocking it. Eric jumped from the vehicle and stumbled away as fast as he could. The explosion temporarily deafened him.

Police cars, ambulances and fire trucks roared to the scene. Fire engulfed the rental car and three nearby cars suffered extensive damage. Eric sat on the ground while EMTs hovered around him, taking his vital signs and asking annoying questions about the day of the week and the name of the President of the United States. After convincing emergency personnel that he was only a little dazed, he sat up and surveyed the devastation. *The rental car company won't be happy. Glad I took out a good insurance package. My adversaries aren't satisfied threatening Sarah's life; they want to end mine too.*

During the commotion, Megan stood talking on her cell phone, trying to reassure her husband that she had not been harmed. When the police interviewed Eric, he told them as much as he dared. He filled out forms, called his insurance agent, and finally reached the rental company. A few hours later, the agency delivered a car to replace the incinerated one. Eric asked if this car had a remote starter and was relieved that it did. Eric needed the technology. He wasn't going to drive another car without a remote. From here on, he would start his car from a distance. He couldn't take chances.

He instructed Megan to call his client and ask to change their appointment, as unforeseen circumstances had caused a delay. The rest of the day passed with no more excitement.

Eric hated waiting, especially when it involved the life of someone he loved. But he knew he must take his time and stand by. Once he knew what to do, he would pounce on a problem and try to solve it. But that could be disastrous if he made the wrong move. Sarah's freedom required careful planning. He could not be a raging bull. It was up to Joseph and God! Eric prayed fervently.

Eric drove home, not wanting an observer to think he would do anything related to freeing Sarah. After an extended nap, he looked at his watch. Joseph's shift would begin in a couple of hours. They spoke by phone and Eric agreed to be at his listening post at the farm. He took great care to avoid being followed.

Chapter 21

*A*fter the late night shift, Eric and Joseph met at their rendezvous. They decided to choose a different café, in case they were being watched. No use allowing for an easy ambush. The wait staff at this 24 hour eatery were glad to have the customers. As usual, Eric would reward them with a generous tip. Such late night visitors could sit wherever they wished. Joseph and Eric always kept their faces toward the door. Unwelcome guests intending them harm must be detected.

Joseph sat down with a heaving sigh. He said a tense atmosphere seemed to hang over the rig crew. Apprehension was hovering in the air like thick smoke. There had been none of the usual banter and good-natured humor that the men usually shared. One roughneck seemed especially uneasy. When Murphy Edwards visited the rig, he pulled this individual aside. They didn't emerge from the mudlogger's shack for a good half hour.

Joseph suggested a bug be placed in the shack. It might prove very instructive! Eric agreed but knew this pushed the envelope a bit too far. He had no authority to officially eavesdrop. But then, lives were dangling dangerously. Sometimes the law got in the way of doing the right thing! Eric warned Joseph not to put himself in serious danger. He feared something sinister might be brewing.

"I will keep a sharp watch on things," Joseph assured Eric. "If things get too hot, I will avoid the burn!" He laughed but with little humor. Their conference ended and both men sought the comfort of sleep to escape the night's pressure. But troubled dreams prevented either from getting much rest. Sarah appeared in Eric's dream again and again as he tossed in bed and worried about her safety.

The next day was blustery, with dark rain clouds. Diverting his attention from the kidnapping, Eric drove to see about Mrs. Flynn's sinkhole problem. Her issue had again slipped his mind with all the action at the rig, and he was delayed with an explosion. The Flynn driveway was slowly sagging into an underground space. Eric brought along a ground-penetrating radar unit to survey the property. The rain let up enough for him to use the instrument easily. After walking the equipment several times across the property, Eric analyzed the data. Readings indicated this might be the only sinkhole on the owner's property. The depression measured several feet deep and eight feet across. Eric estimated the space under the sinkhole was a small cave.

Based on the dimensions of the sinkhole and cave, Eric recommended grouting—that is, filling the space underground with concrete. "That should take care of the problem," he said, "but it isn't a cheap solution. Otherwise your driveway may disappear. I know a firm specializing in such work." He gave the owner a name and phone number for an estimate. Eric would send a bill when he had calculated his time and use of rented equipment. On the way back to his office he felt good about helping someone with a geological problem. How simple that seemed compared to the one he faced as a private investigator!

After the late night shift, Joseph and Eric met at still another café. Joseph sat with bright eyes. Another new roughneck had talked to him during a break. He wanted to know if Joseph would like to earn a little extra cash by helping on a special job. Eric immediately suspected a trap, but Joseph beat him to the conclusion. He already smelled a rodent. "Of course I told him I would be delighted!"

Joseph was to meet the crew member after the next day's shift and travel to the work site. It was an obvious setup. Joseph felt miffed to be considered so stupid that he would fall for the ruse. He and Eric talked about how this might play out.

Eric said, "I wonder if they are looking to use you to lure me into a trap. I've already contacted my friend at the FBI and alerted her about the kidnapping and that you are also a target. She agreed to stay in the background until I call her. The threat on Sarah's life may be real and I don't want to make the criminals uneasy. But now these thugs are involving you. Somehow they want to be certain to get me out of the game. What do you think?"

Joseph said, "I do not know, but I will be careful and do the 'extra work.' I am depending on you to watch my back with that little cell phone and GPS transmitter." He smiled.

"You got it. And I may call in the sheriff or FBI if things get even hotter!" Eric gave Joseph a playful punch on the arm, which made Joseph wince.

"Oh, Joseph, I'm sorry. I forgot about your oil field injury."

As Joseph rubbed his shoulder he said, "One more thing we should discuss is where we meet. I like this café but I think we should keep moving to different places. I wonder if I am being watched. If the company knows we meet anywhere on a regular basis, we could be sitting ducks."

"You got that right! There's another late night café a mile away from here. Let's meet there next time."

"Good idea. See you then!"

After a fitful attempt to sleep, Eric stumbled out of bed. It was Sunday and Eric definitely wanted to attend church. He needed to fortify himself for whatever he had to do to free Sarah.

That night he waited for Joseph's shift to be over so the trip to the "extra work" could be followed.

Eric waited not far from Sarah's house, listening intently to conversation between the roughneck and Joseph as they got into the man's truck and drove to the "extra work." The discussion proved innocuous. Eric heard the pickup stop, followed by a scuffling sound, and then nothing. Something must have happened to the cell phone about a mile from Sarah's farm. The pickup started to move again. Eric went into action, starting his car and heading toward the tiny GPS transmitter's beacon.

To avoid being detected, Eric traveled a road parallel to the pickup. He wasn't certain what to do except follow, since he had lost voice communication. Finally, the pickup stopped. Eric pulled off the road a mile away and waited to see if the truck started moving again. After several minutes of inactivity, he decided to take the offensive.

Removing an electric off-road bike from the trunk of his rental, Eric threw a sniper rifle over his shoulder, checked his Glock, and verified the GPS signal. He knew the area fairly well and could ride to the stopped pickup without being seen or heard. He took off over the fields. Clouds almost extinguished the moonlight, but Eric trusted he could see well enough to avoid crashing into things. Lights were not an option. His GPS unit indicated that the pickup still was not moving.

The ride over the field took a number of minutes. Approaching slowly, he flipped on infrared goggles, which allowed him to see heat glaring clearly from the pickup's engine. Just in time, he saw body images about 50 yards away. *Probably a sniper.* Eric stopped the bike, dismounted, and carefully approached. His night vision glasses picked up a second sniper opposite the first one. Eric did not want to shoot blindly at body heat objects. He must be certain of their identity.

Twenty yards from the first person, Eric breathed a grateful sigh, glad he had not shot a gagged and bound Joseph. Not wanting to arouse the kidnappers, Eric did not attempt to untie Joseph. Instead, he circled around to find the second body heat source. It was Sarah Isaacs, also bound and gagged.

Where are the captors? He had not taken their bait by using the road. Although their trap seemed elaborate, Eric remained undetected—or so it appeared. *I'm still alive.* Fearful that any noise might give away his location, Eric carefully bypassed Sarah. The pickup still glowed brightly, but no other heat signatures showed up. Scanning the area, he noticed a small hill just off the road and opposite the tied captives.

Eric checked for booby traps, trip wires, or other detection equipment as he slowly made a broad circle to skirt the hill's eastern edge. Approaching the back side of the hill, he heard muffled voices. Moving closer he could understand them clearly. One of the men said, "I don't think he's comin'. It don't take this long to come from town."

"Boss said wait and we wait. See?"

Eric made out the two heat sources 25 yards away. No others could be seen. When Eric had crept within 15 yards, he challenged the two men.

"Drop your weapons or you'll never see the sun again!"

The startled men stumbled over each other. One made the mistake of raising his rifle, and Eric shot him in the chest. He dropped with a groan. The other man yelled, "Don't shoot! I ain't no hero. Money won't do me no good if I'm dead!"

"Turn around and drop face down on the ground."

The man quickly obeyed. Eric bound, searched and disarmed him. "Who pays you?"

"Murphy Edwards!"

"Glad to hear it. Now you remember that name when somebody asks you the same question later today."

To Eric's relief, the injured man wasn't dead, but was critically wounded. Killing people weighed heavily on his mind. He was still bothered about shooting the assassin who attacked them at Sarah's farm house. *Why do I have to shoot people? Isn't there a better way to earn a living?* He liked to investigate problems and provide solutions, but sometimes problems involved dangerous individuals wielding guns. *What am I supposed to do?* Tonight he hadn't chosen violence; violence had chosen him. But that didn't help his conscience.

After Eric called the sheriff for officers and an ambulance, he untied the ropes that bound Joseph. Then he went to Sarah to untie her. She had passed out when the shooting started, but she awakened as he loosened the ropes around her body. When Sarah saw Eric, she grabbed him and hugged him as she had never hugged anyone before.

"Oh, Eric! Thank God you came! I thought they would ambush you for certain. I kept praying for you! When I heard shots, I must have fainted."

"Thanks for your prayers. Their ambush setup was amateurish. I guess those thugs expected me to come riding up and shout, 'Here I am, shoot me.'" He laughed, but Sarah did not laugh with him.

Sheriff deputies arrived, gathered data, took testimony, and transported one suspect to the county jail. The wounded suspect was taken by ambulance to the nearest ER. One of the ambulance drivers quipped to Eric, "Haven't seen so much action in my seven years of service. You sure are involved in a lot of stuff." Eric smiled and nodded. *Unfortunately.*

After the sheriff's officers and medics left, Eric, Joseph, and Sarah took refuge at the Isaacs farm. Eric called the FBI to alert them about the kidnapping. They were not happy to be coming into the situation after the fact, but their long association with Eric Bonfield helped smooth the ruffled federal feathers.

Sarah said that the roughneck taken to the hospital was the man who abducted her and held her in a shack not far from the farm. She appeared no worse for wear after enduring days of captivity. Her captors apparently intended her no harm. They kidnapped her to draw Eric into their trap.

Joseph explained that the second thug was hiding in the back of the extended cab. That guy grabbed Joseph from behind. Both thugs bound and gagged him. They found his cell phone and smashed it; then they searched his coat and found the transmitter Eric had sewed into the lining. The assassins left the transmitter in the pickup as a decoy.

"We have to buy a new cell phone," Eric said wryly. "That raises the bill for this case!"

The three laughed nervously; then they turned their attention to the two criminals. If the uninjured one squealed, the case might break wide open—that is, if he didn't back down under questioning. If the two witnesses in jail could implicate Murphy Edwards then Edwards might tell if Arkwell administrators had authorized the crimes.

After their exhausting discussion, they separated to rest. Joseph agreed to return to the oil rig on his next shift as if nothing had happened. Eric suggested that Sarah might be safer at Devon and Fran's house. She agreed but wanted to drive her own car so she could get to work. Eric headed to the sheriff's office with enough evidence, hopefully including the criminal's testimony, to trigger Edward's arrest.

Before going home, Eric made one last call—to the county jail. The officer who booked the uninjured assassin told Eric that he only had so much room for his clients! Eric laughed and asked that this jailbird be kept away from other prisoners, because he didn't want any leak that might trigger an escape by Murphy Edwards. The officer assured Eric that the prisoner would be kept in isolation.

"By the way, Eric, the media are catching wind of all this activity by law enforcement. I don't think any of them know about your involvement. Thought I'd alert you to be wary."

"Thanks. I'll try to stay under the radar." Eric looked at the clock on the wall: 4:30 a.m.! Maybe he could get a few hours' sleep before he went to the office. He drove home to dream of sinkholes, explosions, rifles, and Sarah.

Chapter 22

When Eric arrived at work much later than usual, Megan said, "Eric, this case is beginning to read like a movie script."

"I hope the movie ends soon. It already exceeds the requisite hour and a half-length." They both laughed. He turned to attack the usual stack of work Megan had prepared for him.

Megan said, "You do know the geological consulting business is going very well, don't you?"

"I'm sorry, Megan, I haven't taken time to look at the books lately. It seems I'm busy dodging bullets, escaping exploding cars, and shooting people." He said this grimly.

"Don't worry. I've got your back!"

"You are truly a gem," Eric spoke truthfully.

"By the way," she said, brushing aside the compliment, yet smiling her appreciation, "Your pickup is ready; seems they got it back like new."

"Wonderful! I am so tired of driving a sedan." He left his office and drove to the rental agency. The agent carefully inspected their vehicle for damage. Finding none, he wiped his forehead and said, "Mr. Bonfield, I hope your pickup never has another problem!" Eric grinned and paid his bill.

Although pleased to be back in his pickup, Eric found himself wondering how to break the Arkwell wall of secrecy. He paced the office floor. Megan looked up from her desk. "Eric, there's a man who needs your help. He's about 45 minutes east of here." She handed Eric a sheet of paper. "Why don't you see what you can do for him?" Eric reluctantly read the request. After a few minutes he became intrigued. His enthusiasm renewed, Eric took off and rented some geomagnetic surveying equipment on his way out of town. Megan nodded to herself; she knew how to distract him.

The survey took most of the day, just as Megan thought it would. When Eric dropped off soil samples at an environmental analysis lab, the tech said, "I'm kind of busy but can get you the results in a couple days."

"That's fine. I need to process the magnetic data, and the client doesn't need the report for at least a week." He went to his office to work up the survey information. After a while he looked out the window at the darkened landscape, and this triggered a glance at his watch. "Joseph's shift will be starting in several hours. I'd better get a little rest before it begins." Eric said this out loud, but then realized that Megan had left work hours earlier. He felt sheepish; then he grinned, turned off the light, and walked to the parking lot. There was no explosion and no shot. *What a great night!*

When the late night shift ended without incident, Joseph and Eric conferred at their next café. Joseph was smiling. "Another day, another surveillance. We were short-handed tonight since both those guys who tried to trap you came from my crew. So we did everything without them. I am so tired. Everybody grumbled at the extra work. It just wasn't safe on the rig. And, Edwards didn't show. Finally, another rep came with two very tough looking workers. One of the crew asked the rep, 'Where's Edwards?' After a pause, the rep said, 'Quit.' And that was that."

Eric and Joseph surmised that Edwards had become too much of a liability, especially with some of his employees ready to testify against him. The thug involved in the ambush of Eric had squealed on Murphy Edwards as soon as he was interrogated by sheriff's officers. A search of Edwards' home by sheriff's deputies revealed nothing. He simply had disappeared. No one knew anything about his relatives. It was as if he had never existed. Arkwell Oil Company representatives interviewed by the sheriff knew nothing of his whereabouts. Edwards drifted in, they said, and worked for a few years; then he was gone. If he had hired criminals to do bad things, they knew nothing about it.

After his meeting with Joseph, Eric thought out loud, "These guys are slick. They cover their tracks really well. There must be an opening in their armor somewhere; but where is the chink that could expose those involved with the murders?"

After a nap, Eric called Sarah and asked for an early breakfast date . . . business of course. Eric feared he might be losing focus, what with the kidnaping, shootouts, and disappearance of Edwards. After ordering their meals, he looked into Sarah's beautiful eyes and asked, "Sarah, what do you really hope to discover from this investigation?"

She returned his gaze with sharpened vision and said, "I want to assure myself that Danny's fall was not suicide and, if it wasn't, then I want to find out what or who caused it."

"I understand." Eric paused and then said, "But I suspect there is more. Is there?"

Sarah dropped her eyes and began to sob quietly. "I . . . I . . . feel so guilty! You know those so-called 'royalty checks'? Well, I haven't cashed a single one. As far as I am concerned, they never will be cashed. If those wells had never been dug, Danny might still be alive. It's as if the checks are blood money! I almost feel this 'oil' is blood on my hands . . . Danny's blood! Do you understand?"

Frowning, Eric said, "I see. You feel guilty for receiving money that somehow caused Danny's death."

"Yes! That's exactly how I feel."

"But, Sarah, you know it isn't so. Danny could have died under completely different circumstances on someone else's property."

"I know that. But he died on my property. I don't want any of their filthy money."

Eric began to understand what he had missed earlier. Guilt is not something anyone can argue out of existence. Guilt is guilt. It may be irrational and its origin untrue, but guilt is very real. It defies all truth and logic.

"I'm so sorry, Sarah," he said quietly. "That was insensitive of me. You have every right to be angry. You do need to know what actually happened."

At this she softened and reached for his hand. He enfolded her hand in his and looked again into those hazel eyes filled with tears. He felt sympathy for her, not empathy, since he had never experienced the depth of loss she was feeling. She smiled weakly and said, "Eric, I need you so much."

Eric recalled Megan's advice and checked his emotions. He felt totally incompetent to help Sarah. He smiled and suggested she might talk with her pastor about her feelings.

After breakfast, he took Sarah to her car. He squeezed her hands as they parted, but he did not kiss her. Her facial expression implored him to embrace her, but Eric thought better of it and suggested she really needed to rest after work.

As Eric walked to his pickup, he felt torn up inside. *Did I do the right thing just then? What if I had held Sarah close and kissed her? Would that have helped her? Was it passion she needed to help her through this guilt-driven time in her life? I am clueless. I hope Sarah will talk with her pastor. A professional minister might know what to say or how to direct Sarah to some resolution. I hope so.*

Eric drove to his apartment with his mind dancing back and forth between his feelings for Sarah, Megan's story of her relationship with her husband, and where to take the investigation from here. Sensing no resolution about his relationship to Sarah or how to proceed with the case, he decided he needed guidance himself.

After work at the office and a quick supper, Eric went to his apartment. He prayed that God would give him clear direction. Afterwards, he read an inspirational book. Eventually he dropped off to sleep, and the book fell gently from the bed to the floor. His alarm awoke him to check on Joseph. Eric felt no fresh insights. *That's the way some days begin, or in this case nights. I need even one idea to crack this investigation snag.* None had come by overnight express.

Out on Sarah's farm nothing amiss had happened. Another well reached "target" and the rig moved to a different location. Joseph called Eric and wondered if the company had been frightened into silence. Not so, as he found out after his shift ended.

On his way home, Joseph caught a glimpse of a pickup behind him. He spoke into his cell phone and said, "Looks like a tail."

"I'm on my way. Stay on the main road and don't let him pass you."

Joseph sped up. The tail sped up, too, and gained a little. "Not looking good," Joseph said.

They flew down the county road at least 20 miles above the speed limit. When Joseph spotted a cross-road coming up on the right, he decided on an evasive maneuver and slid the car sideways, throwing gravel as he turned onto the side road. Following too closely behind, the tail lost control and the pickup rolled over and over, scattering a cloud of rocks and dust.

"Eric," Joseph said into the hidden cell phone, "the tail just took a tumble."

"I'm close to your GPS location. Slow down and let's see who's in the pickup."

Joseph stopped and turned around as Eric came into view. The tailing truck sat on its top with wheels still spinning. Gasoline spewed from a ruptured tank. The occupants seemed unable to get out. Joseph and Eric parked at safe distances away and rushed to the truck. Inside the cab two men were unconscious. Their safety airbags had malfunctioned and the men looked in bad shape.

"Quick, cut them out of their seat belts before this truck explodes," yelled Eric. The hunting knives they always carried with them flashed and bit through tough belt material, releasing the captives. Eric and Joseph yanked the men free and dragged them a safe distance just as gasoline touched the hot engine and ignited. Flames erupted and engulfed the vehicle in an inferno. Joseph and Eric shielded themselves from the searing heat and dragged the unconscious men further away. Eric called the sheriff.

"Eric, who do you have now?" the sheriff asked.

"Oh, I just thought you needed more guys for your jail!" Eric joked grimly.

When an ambulance arrived, the EMTs shook their heads at seeing Eric and Joseph again. "Keepin' us busy! But, hey, at least we can take these to the hospital and not the morgue!"

Fire fighters eventually extinguished the blaze. When the wreckage had cooled enough, Eric and Joseph, along with deputies, examined the remains. They found two sniper rifles, barely recognizable, partially incinerated hand guns, and the remains of a satellite phone. Eric supposed the assassins had used the phone in rural areas without cell phone reception.

At the ER, doctors pronounced both men critical with serious skull injuries. Their survival was not certain. Joseph wondered how many thugs Arkwell Oil Company had on their payroll.

Eric said, with a touch of sarcasm, "They must run a continuous want ad in the Criminal Gazette." Then he became serious. "Joseph, I'm concerned for your safety."

Joseph protested, "Hey, I kind of like the excitement. I'm good to continue." Eric grudgingly agreed to another try. This one would prove even more dangerous.

The following night, when his shift ended, Joseph saw the two workers who had recently been added to the crew standing by his car. They were tough-looking men, and he wondered what they were up to. He spoke into the cell phone and warned Eric, who was on stakeout at Sarah's farm, his pickup out of sight in the garage.

"On the way," said Eric.

Approaching his car, Joseph quietly acknowledged them with a single word: "Gentlemen."

"Where do you think you is goin', José?"

"I beg your pardon," Joseph calmly responded. "I think you mistake me for my cousin. He is in Mexico. My name is not José."

"Don't care what your name is. Git in the truck." Stalling for time, Joseph asked what they had in mind.

"None of your business, Spaniard!"

"You keep mistaking who I am, Señor."

One of the burly men advanced toward Joseph, and Joseph took a step backward to avoid his grasp. Together, the two thugs leaped at Joseph. Little did they know Joseph had been a boxer in Mexico before immigrating to the United States. Light on his feet, Joseph leaped to the side and, as he did, landed a wicked hook to the jaw of the closest man, who went down with a thud. The second man was so shocked at the fall of his partner that he did not block Joseph's blow to his head. Both were out cold before Eric arrived.

Eric spoke into his phone, "Sounds like you didn't need me!"

"Sí, these guys are really dumb. No problem." He was rubbing his hand.

Joseph went back to the rig and told the tool pusher about the incident. Their boss huffed and walked over to the unconscious men, who lay in a heap. He prodded them with his boot. "Get up you (a string of epithets followed)."

They eventually roused themselves, shook their heads and massaged their bruises. "Now get out of here and don't come back!" the crew leader yelled. They scrambled to their feet and made for their pickup. The boss turned to Joseph and said the men would be fired. And it was so!

A short time later, Eric and Joseph met at still another café. Fortunately, Little Rock features a number of late night places to eat.

"This is too much," Eric said. "We'd better call a halt to your surveillance, Joseph. What is gained by drawing the ire of these people?"

Joseph said, "I know, but let's go ahead anyway. Besides, I like the pay! And, get this, the company rep who replaced Murphy Edwards called me to the mudlogger's shack and apologized for the trouble with these guys. He wanted to make it up to me by working on the completed wells. The work is not as heavy as on the rig."

"That is interesting! Any ideas about this?"

"I was puzzled at first but agreed to try it. I'll be on well #2 tomorrow morning. This is a day shift when the tankers come and go. Maybe something might happen on the rig and they didn't want me to see it. Or maybe they will try some other stunt on the 'producing' well."

Eric said, "I'll be at the farm house observing all the action with binoculars."

As Joseph rose to go, Eric asked, "Joseph, you seem to be relatively unphased by the risks you are taking. Do you mind telling me why this is?"

Joseph became serious and said, "Eric, where I come from we take risks for our families all the time. It is part of providing for them. Risks are part of life."

Nodding, Eric said, "You are amazing, my friend."

"Maybe a little crazy, but not amazing!" Joseph laughed.

That morning, after only a brief break to rest, Joseph found the crew at the next well even more surly than the two jokers who had tried to jump him. "Not a happy group," Joseph spoke quietly into his cell phone.

The first tanker of the day pulled in and connected to the well pipe. Joseph watched as something flowed into the well. The smell was awful. Once the tank was empty, the truck rumbled away.

Joseph told Eric via phone, "The rep told the truth; this job is easy. But I don't think the product being pumped into the well is good."

Truck after truck arrived and repeated the process. Joseph knew better than to ask questions. He simply did his job and quietly observed everything.

At shift's end, the crew suddenly became jovial and talked about going into town for a drink. They invited Joseph to join them. Someone said, "Hey, let's all go in our trucks." Joseph thanked them but said he would drive behind them in his own car, since he did not know the way. They pressed him to ride with them but Joseph politely declined.

"I will join you at the bar," he said firmly. "You lead the way. I must visit a relative right after, and I don't have time to come back for my car."

The crew muttered but agreed to the arrangement. Joseph made certain his vehicle took up the caboose position, behind the parade. He stayed just far enough away to avoid any funny business. Eric trailed behind Joseph and poised himself to join in if things got messy. Apparently Joseph had foiled their plan by driving himself. Eric wondered if there would have been another hijacking, resulting in Joseph's demise.

Arriving at the bar, the blustery crowd poured out of their pickups and jostled their way inside. Joseph discretely parked his car out in the open away from other vehicles so that any tampering would not go unnoticed.

Joseph walked into the bar and sat at a table with three other men. They all joked and laughed. Joseph knew that a bar is a perfect setup for a knife fight or other brawl where someone gets hurt. He kept his back to the wall so he could see everything going on around him. Suddenly Eric appeared at the door! Joseph smiled inwardly as Eric walked over to Joseph's table and asked if he could sit down. The other crew members agreed. They did not recognize Eric.

A ruckus began as two crew members began pushing each other. The shoving turned nasty and moved toward Joseph and Eric's table. Guessing the plan, Eric and Joseph quickly moved aside as the two brawlers landed on the table. Cat-like, Eric and Joseph were out the door before someone yelled and the roughnecks rushed outside. The crowd spilled out and everyone looked for Joseph. Seeing him get into his car, they ran toward him as he started the engine and sped out of the parking lot. Cursing, they watched the car disappear around a corner. Eric smiled, ambled to his truck, opened the door, got in, and drove away from the dumbfounded workers.

Chapter 23

*J*oseph and Eric gathered at another new rendezvous. They laughed nervously about the bar escapade. It was clear Arkwell Oil would not stop until they had eliminated all threats to their enterprise. Eric now had enough evidence to ask state authorities to inspect the wells. This could shut down the operation, but it would ignore the apparent murder of employees who had tried to blow the whistle on Arkwell. In addition, closing the operation would leave the death of Danny Isaacs, Eric's first obligation as a private investigator, unsolved. The attempted murders of Joseph and himself didn't implicate the company either. The only person ranking higher than an oil rig crew member who could be charged had disappeared into thin air. Murphy Edwards no longer existed.

Eric was tired of the amateurish attempts on his and Joseph's lives. Yet these failures only seemed to reinforce the company's resolve to kill them. *Is it time to change tactics and confront Arkwell Oil Company staff head on?* But how could they get someone high in the company to play their hand and open a crack in the system?

Eric and Joseph decided to sleep on it and return to their deliberations the next day. Driving home, Eric realized he should contact Sarah and bring her up to date. Maybe discussing things with her would give rise to some new ideas. Right now, he felt drained of creativity. He dialed her number. "How about some dinner this evening after work with an exhausted P.I.?" he asked.

"I'd love to!"

They met at Antonio's. Where else? Eric just could not get enough of their wonderful Italian fare.

When they were seated, Sarah said, "I took your advice and talked with my pastor. His insights helped. I feel a little less guilt for Danny's death. But I still resent allowing a drill rig on my property. And I have to learn the truth about Danny's death. I want to know what happened and why."

Eric breathed a huge sigh of relief and took her hands in his. She smiled and squeezed his in return. Something unspoken passed between them, something that did not require words.

After Sarah heard Eric's outline of the latest attempts on Joseph's life, she said with worry in her voice, "They are so persistent, Eric; I'm concerned for Joseph's safety. Does he have to take so many risks?" After a pause, she turned the discussion a new direction. "Eric, what sort of evidence is needed to convict the company staff of serial murder?"

Eric blinked and snapped his fingers. "Sarah, you are right. I need to focus on what actually happened to the missing workers!" He jerked out his cell phone and called one of his fellow private investigators whose specialty was missing persons. "Henry? Eric Bonfield here. Listen. I need some hard data on missing persons. I can give you names. Their whereabouts may be critical to a large case I'm working on. Yes, I can send them from my phone."

Sarah watched as Eric feverishly punched the names of missing roughnecks into his cell phone. Then he gulped the last of his food and escorted Sarah to her car. He thanked her, squeezed her hand, gave her a light peck on the lips, and dashed off.

Dazed, Sarah stared after Eric's retreating truck. *So much for a romantic dinner! Eric is a great guy, but at times he gets awfully distracted.*

Eric drove home, pulled out his notebook, and started jotting down possible explanations for the missing roughnecks. Murder? An obvious choice. What else? Kidnapping? Possible, but where were the men now? Had they been bought off to keep their mouths shut? Maybe, but where did they all disappear to?

The following morning Eric beat the alarm. He managed a quick breakfast on the way to the office and began receiving a portfolio of information about each of the missing workers. His fax machine hummed, tumbling out sheet after sheet of police reports and missing persons' data on each name. Eric thanked God for people like Henry who specialize and can find information fast. *Why didn't I think of this sooner?* Eric smiled ruefully, knowing that "why" questions rarely have good answers!

The fax machine churned out enough information to keep Eric busy for the rest of the day. All the names bore a common thread: they were all blue collar workers who had disappeared while working in Arkwell oil fields. None had an obituary and no bodies had ever been found. *I hope this absence of data rules out murder.*

A few reports suggested that some of the missing men were now living outside the United States, specifically in Mexico. Rumors had surfaced that some individuals, although still alive, were not permitted to leave Mexico. One roughneck had managed to send a message to his parents, but "Details on the contents of the message remain unknown." Eric jumped from his chair and frantically punched in the phone number of the parents.

"Hello, Mrs. Jockem? My name is Eric Bonfield. I'm a private investigator and am looking for missing persons. Could I come and ask some questions?" The parents of Edmund Jockem anxiously agreed, and Eric raced to the address, which was about an hour away. When he arrived at the small one-story frame house from the 1950s, Edmunds parents were waiting, cautiously hopeful, on the front stoop.

Eric introduced himself, "I'm Eric Bonfield. Thank you for letting me speak with you. I understand that Edmund worked in the oil fields. Do you know the name of the most recent company he worked for?"

"Arkwell Oil."

What else could it be? "How about the circumstances right before your son came up missing?"

Mrs. Jockem, who spoke English better than her husband, controlled the conversation. "Edmund spoke to us about some irregularities at the drilled wells. He said he planned to talk with police; that was the last we heard from him."

"Did you report that he was missing to the police?"

"Yes. An officer came and asked some questions. We waited a few weeks but never heard from anyone. We are poor people. We didn't know what to do. So we prayed and waited some more."

What she said upset Eric. "You didn't hear anything more from the police?"

"No, nothing."

If an important person went missing, the treatment would be different. Eric was certain of that. *I wonder if the questionable police captain in Precinct 2 was also involved in cutting off this investigation.* Arkwell Oil must use the same method to quiet anyone with suspicions about their operation. Any potential whistle-blower would find himself on a missing persons list. With a high level mole inside police headquarters, it would be easy to stifle an investigation.

"But I understand you received a communication from Edmund. Is that true?"

"Yes," Mrs. Jockem said. "We did hear from him. It was indirect. It seems he was able to bribe someone to send a text message. I still have it in this desk." She opened a drawer and carefully removed a small slip of paper with some handwriting on it. "Here it is."

Eric gingerly took the precious document from her shaking fingers. It read: "Confined to zinc mine in Mexico near Aux . . . ." The remaining smudged letters could not be deciphered. Mrs. Jockem apologized for the smudges; she had tried to write out the words but the ink had smeared. Unfortunately, the text message had been sent to a friend's phone and was deleted.

She said again that she and her husband did not know what to do. Calls to the police went unanswered. She hoped to hear more from Edmund, but nothing appeared. She kept the only connection with their son in a drawer. All that she knew about her son resided on that tiny piece of paper.

Eric felt a moment of frustration, but paused, remembering a friend who restored distorted or faded writing. "Mrs. Jockem, may I take this to an expert to see if it can be returned to clarity? I promise you will get it back."

Mrs. Jockem replied eagerly, "Yes! We have nothing to lose."

Eric's friend, Samantha, was known for her work with poorly preserved documents to make them readable. Eric could hardly wait to get to her office.

"Always worth a try," Samantha said. "Let me see what I can do. Will you wait?" She viewed the damaged writing by using infrared and ultraviolet light combined with computer-assisted software; slowly, legible writing appeared. About an hour later, she announced the best result: ". . . zinc mine in Mexico near Auxolo." She searched online and suggested Auxolo might be a town. Of course, it might not be a town, but an arroyo, a small river, a mountain or some cultural feature.

Auxolo, what secrets do you hold? Eric phoned the Jockem family to let them know what he learned from the search. It was a faint lead—but it was a lead that Eric could follow up on.

Eric met Joseph after his shift. Joseph reported that the crew members had apologized for their rowdiness at the bar and hoped he would join them again. But he looked wearily at Eric. "You know, I am getting tired of dodging bullets and these people."

When Eric told him what he had learned about the missing persons, Joseph perked up and said, "This is good news; not everyone on the list has been murdered! Someone is alive! But how can this Edmund Jockem be found?"

"I've done a deep search of a geological database on Mexican zinc resources. The search revealed three zinc sites associated with the word Auxolo. If Auxolo is the name of a town, then we might have only one place to search."

"We . . . search?" Joseph replied quizzically.

"Certainly. You and me. If we find Edmund Jockem alive, he's probably with the others. We solve a missing person's case and shut down Arkwell Oil for good."

Joseph stared at Eric.

"Oh, I'm sorry, Joseph. We'll both need to go since my Spanish is rather limited."

Joseph shrugged. "I guess I'll ask for a leave from the company. It won't hurt my feelings to be out of there." Then, after some thought, he added, "It would be dangerous to announce my leaving at the beginning of the shift. I will drive back to the rig and speak to my boss now. That way there won't be a chance of hatching another plot against me."

When Joseph asked about a leave, his boss appeared cautious, even unwilling, but he caught himself. "Yes, of course you may. What do you plan to do?"

"I would like to visit my family. I have not seen them for some time." Although a true statement, it covered the real reason for leaving. "May I have my job back when I return?"

"Of course, by all means; you are a good worker."

Joseph drove by back roads to reach town. With no time for the company to lay a trap, he made it safely to Eric's apartment. He and Eric knew they must leave quickly and head for the border. No use giving Arkwell any chance of guessing their plan.

"What else do we need for this rescue operation?" Eric wondered out loud. "Let's see. I have a list with the names of the twelve missing men. Oh, yes. We need food, water, gas, and firepower. Armed security guards probably watch the roughnecks."

Joseph wondered how they could move weapons across the border, but he assumed Eric would find some way.

Chapter 24

Eric made several phone calls. He had done favors for others in the world of crime investigation at the federal and state level, and now he needed a favor from them—expect a crowd of U.S. citizens exiting Mexico without passports and maybe without identification. His contact friend at the FBI helped prepare the way for this unusual group crossing.

"I feel like an undercover agent in a movie," Joseph said. "You really do know a lot of people."

"Got to in the P.I. business, if you ever want help. I've developed relationships with many people in law enforcement. I helped some folk in Texas find criminals wanted for crimes against the U.S. government, and now I'm calling in a favor to let us help some slaves exit Mexico."

Joseph just shook his head. *This guy has so many connections!*

The border crossing took several hours but went much smoother than the rest of the trip. Once across the line separating the two independent countries, Eric drove to a location known only to a few persons. He had called a contact in Mexico to gather weapons they might need to free the roughnecks. No way could they have taken any arms across the border. When they were finished with the guns, these well-chosen items would be returned to their owners, along with some cash in appreciation.

After a day of travel in Mexico, they were on a road leading toward one of the Auxolo sites. It proved anything but easy—unpaved rural Arkansas roads are interstates compared to this remote part of Mexico. Finally, they found the dirt road to a town named Auxolo. After bouncing along, the

GPS indicated Auxolo lay just ahead. It could hardly be called a town. Aside from a Catholic church and three bars, Auxolo offered little else.

Joseph and Eric hit bartenders with questions about zinc mines. They learned that two of the Auxolo sites produced such measly amounts of zinc that nobody bothered with them anymore. However, a strange assortment of workers scratched out a living at a third small operation. This information piqued Eric's attention.

One bartender said, "Most miners who come to my bar look like Americans. They spend a little money for beer, but that is all." He smiled. "The mine must not produce much ore, since the miners have so little to spend."

Hearing that the mining crew consisted of Americans with little money caused Eric to jump out of his chair. Maybe a breakthrough lay just ahead! Getting directions to the mine, he and Joseph headed over rutted, narrow roads, stopping a quarter mile from the mine to avoid detection. Walking the rest of the way by a circuitous path made them feel like mountain goats.

The sun was high in the sky and temperatures kept pace. Sweat poured off the two men. When the mine came into view, they saw people moving in and out of a tunnel that had been dug into the mountainside. Using steamy field glasses, they surveyed the site, expecting to see heavy security, but no guards were visible. Maybe they were escaping the day's heat by staying inside. Ore was coming out of the mine on makeshift push-rail cars bumping over an irregular narrow gauge track.

Eric and Joseph watched as two workers pushed a car out of the tunnel and dumped the contents onto a pile at the base of a steep slope. A return set of tracks wound its way back to the tunnel so another car could take its load to the pile. After watching the proceedings for a while, Eric and Joseph saw no change. The workers lacked any constraints on their legs or arms. They moved freely and the tone of their voices did not suggest forced labor. *Puzzling.* Finally, Eric and Joseph moved into the open and walked to the tunnel entrance just as another car emerged. The two workers jumped at the strangers' appearance and held up their hands.

"Hey, we know we ain't got no permit but we're willin' to pay you. Just don' tell the police!" one of them called out in a decidedly Midwestern accent.

His response caught Joseph and Eric off guard. "We're not here to collect a bribe or arrest anyone," Eric said. "We're looking for Edmund Jockem."

The workers looked at each other in bewilderment. "No such person here by that name. What'd you want 'im for"?

"We thought he worked as a slave in a mine near here." At this, both of the miners laughed out loud. Another working pair emerged, and they, too, seemed equally shocked at the statement.

One of the workers said, "Everybody here is an import from the States. We formed us an unofficial corporation to mine this stuff. We're here to make a fast buck and ditch the place. Ya can't get a hamburger or anythin' worth drinkin' out here."

Eric and Joseph were crestfallen. "Are there any other Americans working zinc deposits near here?"

The four men looked uncertain until a third group emerged. One of these workers was more helpful. "I think you guys got your location wrong. There's lots of places by the name of Auxolo in this part of Mexico. The only other zinc mines are over on the Auxolo River, if you can call it a river. More like an expanded arroyo, I'd say." He explained how to reach the area. It would take a good day's drive over terrain that would make the road to the first Auxolo seem like a boulevard.

Eric and Joseph groaned inwardly at the prospect of such a trek, but maybe they would find the lost roughnecks. They wished the miners well and started on an arduous journey. At least they didn't have to worry about gas; Eric had stowed several extra cans of fuel in the pickup. Feeling philosophical, Joseph said, "You know, Eric, all of life is a journey, and sometimes the hardest part is the most rewarding." Eric nodded despondently as they drove toward whatever lay ahead.

They bounced several miles down the road, trying unsuccessfully to avoid potholes. Joseph remarked that his teeth were jarring so much he needed one of those mouth guards NFL players wear.

"Hope my springs hold up," Eric said. "We bottom out every other pothole. It is beautiful country, though."

Their GPS unit helped them keep on the right track; not that there were many other roads to choose from. Of course, calling the route a road was a bit of a stretch. They would need the GPS to even hope to find their way back!

They were about half-way to their destination when the sharp crack of a rifle stunned them to silence and a bullet stung a nearby boulder.

Eric moaned, "Are we going to be ambushed out here?" Then he actually brightened at the thought since these might be Arkwell Oil people.

A voice shouted in English, "Stop where you are. That was just a warning. You are trespassing on private property."

Eric shouted back, "We're just passing through and didn't know about any private land. Can we talk?"

"Wait there," the voice answered.

They sat in their pickup for ten minutes while the shooter climbed down from an observation post. The man carried a wicked looking rifle; his countenance was grim.

"What's your business," he demanded.

"We're just headed toward the Auxolo River. Didn't know this . . . er . . . road passed through land that belonged to anyone."

"Auxolo River, eh? That's the most desolate spot in this part of Mexico. You can't be going there to find a resort spa!" He laughed.

Eric and Joseph chuckled at his joke. "No, we're interested in zinc and hear there may be some prospects there," said Eric.

"Zinc! Oh, yeah. There's a broken-down surface mine over there where some guys are trying to scratch out some zinc ore. My advice is to turn around and try somewhere else. This is hard scrabble country."

Eric cleared his throat. "Don't mind telling us what you use your land for?"

"This is my personal retreat. I hate close quarters and this is wide open country here. I'm here to be alone. Enough said?"

Eric said, "I respect a man's desire for solitude and like it myself, but is it all right if my friend and I move on to the Auxolo River?"

The man considered this a minute, then waved them on. Eric and Joseph both thanked him for his hospitality. When well out of earshot, Joseph turned to Eric and said, "That is some strange guy, if you don't mind me saying so!"

Eric agreed. He maneuvered around another rut in the so-called road. The delay with the stranger had cost them time. They'd never be able to reach the river before dark.

"Looks like we'll have to sleep under the stars again, amigo," Joseph observed.

"Yep," Eric laughed. "I'm afraid there aren't any Hilton Inns out here."

Pulling off at one of the few flat areas next to the road, they snacked on leftovers. Joseph looked up as the stars began to turn on. The rising moon added a ghostly hue to the rugged landscape of steep hills and boulders. He asked, without expecting an answer, "Why choose this place to hide a bunch of oil field roughnecks?" Eric shook his head. He had no idea.

Exhausted from the rough ride, they turned in for the night by sleeping in the flat bed of the truck. Snoozing on the ground in rattlesnake country had no appeal to them. Eric's pickup had a nice cover over the bed, which offered some protection from marauding creatures that prowled these dry mountains by night. The air quickly turned chilly in this high country; the cover felt good.

Morning came, as usual in this area, dry and bright. They managed a brief breakfast and drove, if that is the correct term, toward the river, trying to cover as much distance as possible before the heat became stifling. About mid-morning they approached something like a river bed. It was dry at this season of the year, except for occasional brief but intense downpours that swelled the stream into flash floods. "We must keep an eye on the sky," Joseph remarked, wary of the danger of such storms. Eric nodded.

They reached the river's steep bank, but no open pit mine greeted them. Eric pulled up a map of the area on his satellite phone and guessed where to search. A small, light-colored patch on the map might be the mine. The map suggested they follow a rude path just wide enough for the pickup. *Ultra-rural roads.* Travel conditions had gone from bad to awful to terrible. Topping a rise, Eric quickly braked to a stop. In the distance a wisp of smoke rose.

"Bingo!" Eric said excitedly. They cautiously drove on. Stopping well short of the smoke, Eric said, "Better walk from here."

"Sí," said Joseph.

Keeping low hills in front of them and following small arroyos to minimize exposure, at last they peered over a ridge and saw what Eric had expected to see at the previous mine. Guards stood at post around a group of men who worked with pick and shovel. Joseph whispered. "I don't think these are law enforcement officers!"

Eric nodded.

Joseph again whispered, "What is the plan?"

Eric shrugged and whispered back, "I'm thinking . . . and praying; how about you?"

Joseph smiled back. They needed both thought and prayer to pull off this rescue and survive in the process.

They lay in a shallow arroyo for half an hour assessing the strength of the guards. Only three were visible, covering at least a dozen miners. Eric knew that he and Joseph could pick off the guards, but he hated the idea of bloodshed. Joseph pointed to a deep arroyo that ran between them and the guards. The guards stood with backs to that arroyo. If the pair could get in position, they might get the drop on the guards and avoid shooting anyone.

Slowly they moved around to the mouth of the arroyo and inched their way up the steep incline. The rough gravel and sand gnawed at their clothing as they crawled higher and higher. Before arriving at a defensible position to surprise the guards, one of the armed men came to the edge of the ravine to relieve himself. Eric and Joseph froze as they tried to look like part of the scenery, but to no avail.

"Hey, who's down there?" the guard yelled, as he raised his rifle. Joseph shot first, and the guard toppled into the arroyo as his rifle discharged harmlessly.

Their cover blown, Eric and Joseph rose from the arroyo and yelled, almost in unison, "Drop your weapons or you'll get what your friend got." The other two guards did as they were told, and Eric breathed a sigh. He wanted no more bloodletting.

Eric and Joseph climbed out of the arroyo. While Joseph covered the guards, Eric walked toward the workers, who were holding their hands in the air, their teeth chattering.

Eric asked, "Is Edmund Jockem in this group?"

A young man answered unsteadily, "That would be me, I reckon."

"Good. Don't worry. We aren't here to harm you. Call us the rescue party. We assume you want to be rescued. Is that right?"

At this the miners lowered their hands and let out a cheer!

Joseph and Eric searched the guards and found papers implicating Arkwell Oil. The names of the missing men matched those on Bodien's list. Eric felt relief to learn there were a dozen fewer murders than he had imagined. He photographed the site, the guards, and the former slave workers. At last, Eric had evidence to use in court.

The injured guard was not in serious shape. They bandaged him so he could travel. Eric offered a prayer and thanked God they had found all the missing roughnecks alive.

The men broke camp, piled into company trucks, and drove away from a living death. The guards would make excellent witnesses at trials of the Arkwell Oil cadre.

As they traveled toward the Mexico/Texas border, the roughnecks began telling Eric and Joseph their stories. Each had recognized the illegality of the wells Arkwell drilled under the ruse of oil prospecting. When management realized they might spill the truth to state authorities, each was systematically captured, drugged, and taken to this desolate place. Some put up a fight when Bodien tried to grab them. That accounted for the nicks and bruises Jean described on Bodien. The ore grade zinc yielded a decent profit for Arkwell, since the men worked without pay! Ah, the joys of a diversified business!

Joseph had discovered a route around the hermit's property, so the return to the border took less time than the journey from the border to the Auxolo mine. On the way Eric returned the weapons to his friend, along with words of appreciation and money. They were glad for both but smiled most while counting the cash.

There was a lot of explaining at the border to get back across with the prisoners and roughnecks, but Eric's phone calls had worked their magic. At the border they were met by a bevy of state and federal law enforcement folk. Once on U.S. soil, the roughnecks all shouted for joy and clapped each other on their backs.

After giving sworn testimony to the FBI and sheriff's representatives, the roughnecks were allowed to return to Arkansas but were instructed to remain quiet, stay at their homes, and avoid fanfare. No use tipping off the Arkwell Oil crowd before the law leaped on the criminals. The guards were in jail, ready for detailed interrogation and safe keeping.

Eric and Joseph returned to their apartments and fell into bed, each sleeping close to twelve hours straight. When they were, at last, ready for a new day's events, Joseph decided not to return to his old employer.

Eric called Sarah but got no answer, so he drove to the safe house, assuming he would find her there. Nobody answered his knock. Concerned, he forced open the back door and found the place in shambles. A large note pinned to a wall read, "If you even think of starting something, we have all three of your friends. Their futures are in your hands."

Eric collapsed in a heap onto a broken chair, which almost shattered under his weight. Had Arkwell Oil learned about the slave camp raid? Had there been a plant in the work crew who leaked information? Had one of the released captives accidently let out the story of their rescue? Or maybe Arkwell hadn't heard about the raid on the slave pit. *Either way, this is a desperate attempt to quiet me.* Details didn't matter right now; Eric's three friends, Sarah, Devon, and Fran, had been kidnapped!

Chapter 25

Eric had more than enough evidence to bring down the company and its terrible work. Somebody would probably be convicted of murder! But now three more lives faced danger . . . lives he cared a great deal about.

After a few minutes of self-pity, Eric straightened up and looked around the disheveled house. *Maybe, just maybe, a clue is hidden in the rubble. A forensic team and Joseph's sharp eye might help me get past my emotions.* He pulled out his cell phone and dialed the sheriff first, then Joseph.

While he waited, Eric assessed the damage. The house was a wreck. It was obvious that Sarah and his two friends hadn't gone quietly. When the sheriff's team and Joseph arrived, they all searched the house thoroughly, hoping to find at least a scrap of a clue. They found nothing that identified the abductors.

Unlike the bumbling group that had kidnapped Sarah earlier, this sophisticated gang must have used gloves. They left no fingerprints; there wasn't even the slightest clue. The forensics team found nothing to go on. "Must have been professionals," the leader observed.

Eric called his friend at the FBI. Federal and sheriff officials would start the search for Arkwell Oil executives as soon as search warrants were released. Eric pleaded for enough time to find his friends.

His FBI contact said, "Look Eric, this whole thing is totally out of hand. You need us to help."

"I know . . . I know! But I'm afraid that their lives are really in danger this time. Let me try a less frontal approach."

After the forensics personnel left, Eric and Joseph stared at the ransacked house. Then Joseph said, "Eric, didn't you give Sarah a small transmitter after the first kidnapping?"

Eric brightened, "Yes! I did. And we didn't find it during the search. I'll bet Sarah has it with her, and it might be turned on." He snatched his cell phone and turned on the app. Sure enough, a signal located Sarah's transmitter.

"Joseph, you are a genius!" He grabbed Joseph and hugged him, man style.

"Eric, you are the one who gave it to her. Can you tell where she is?"

Eric looked at the screen. "Not at the farm. These guys are serious. They've taken them to the next county west. It doesn't look like they're moving. I've got a friend in the sheriff's department in that county. I'll alert him to be ready."

Joseph gave a sigh. "Well, what are we waiting for?"

On their way out of town, they stopped at Eric's office to pick up equipment and firearms. This group might not be easy to catch off guard, especially if they had been warned of the raid in Mexico. Tossing everything they might need into the pickup, Eric and Joseph sped toward the blinking source. The signal grew stronger the closer they got to the county seat. Surely Arkwell wasn't keeping the three hostages in town! That seemed odd, but maybe it was intentional. He and Joseph must be prepared for anything.

As they wove their way through downtown streets, Eric wondered what tactics would be needed to release the prisoners. He was used to rural sites with natural vegetation and landscape cover. Here, buildings, walls, closets, and other inconveniences complicated any search.

Joseph was watching the map closely so he could tell Eric which way to turn. At last they slowed and Joseph pointed to an old brick building in a run-down section of the city. It sat isolated, not touching any adjacent buildings. "Must be an urban renewal project," Eric said. At least they knew where the signal came from. Too bad the open area provided no cover to sneak up to the building.

Eric called the local sheriff but asked her to wait until a plan could be devised to rescue his friends. Storming the bastille didn't seem like a good idea. Eric feared for Sarah and his friends' lives. Gunplay might end up hurting innocent people.

They parked a block away and surveyed the area. Eric said, "Not going to be as easy as the raid in Mexico, or the rescue of you and Sarah that night in a field."

Joseph pointed to an old culvert, partly broken, that led up to the building. Would that let them approach unnoticed? They might reach an exterior door, but this obvious entrance might be booby-trapped; it looked too inviting. Was there another way?

Further searching revealed a collapsed fire escape at one side of the building. It wasn't much but, if they could get to it, there might be enough cover to get to a door. No other means of entering the building seemed likely, except the most dangerous: rush the place and take cover in a doorway. Nothing looked good. Daytime provided maximum visibility. Night afforded cover, but infrared goggles turned people into torch lights!

Then, as Joseph thumbed through a local website, he found a reference to a parade celebrating the town's centennial. It was scheduled for that afternoon. The parade route wove its way by two sides of the building where Sarah and Eric's friends waited for rescue. If Joseph and Eric became part of the parade, they might slide out of the festivities and reach a door without being noticed.

The parade would begin in an hour. That gave them time to find clothing to hide their weapons and whatever they imagined they might need once inside. A visit to a local party supply store yielded baggy clown suits that covered their gear. After donning their apparel, they stared at each other and laughed!

Waiting in anticipation, they considered the options. Doors to the building which held Sarah, Devon, and Fran faced all four directions. Eric planned to sidle out of the parade on the west side, and Joseph, the north. Were sentries posted at each door? Were the doors rigged with explosives or alarms? Those possible dangers had to be faced.

They hoped that the noise of the parade might be enough to cover any sound they would make upon entering the building. Could they force their way in and surprise the guards? Once they were inside, then what? Eric and Joseph each prayed for guidance and safety for all involved. Then they moved into the parade crowd and began one of the longest marches of their lives, or at least it felt like it.

The parade was a hodge-podge of floats, bands, clowns, random street performers and the general public who liked to show off. Joining the crowd three blocks away from their target gave Eric and Joseph time to perfect their act. They both hammed it up and found ready acceptance by the boisterous throng. Approaching the building, Eric glanced up from time to time to assess the environment. Lots of small windows dotted the five-story structure. Recessed doorways provided visual shelter for anyone who made it to a door. It would be impossible for anyone on the upper floors to see them, once they were in a doorway.

Slowly the crowd shuffled along. Joseph and Eric each perspired inside the heavy clown outfits as they approached their entry points. Eric would leave the crowd first and make for a doorway without fanfare. He must look casual and appear involved in the parade. He wondered if the guards were in a heightened state of alertness; or maybe they were more relaxed while watching goofy people march by. Joseph bore his persona well, staying alert and calm. He, too, glanced up to see if the windows carried faint shadows of lookouts. The parade passed the building and turned.

Eric's heart beats increased as his part of the group neared his assigned door. Only 10 yards from the entrance! He told himself to get ready. Then the parade came to a halt; an axle on one of the floats had broken. Everyone milled around, eager to continue. Was this delay unfortunate or an opportunity? If Eric wandered over to the doorway now he might go unnoticed. But if he made a racket while opening the door, the crowd might stare and give away his position to an observer. Eric decided that wisdom and valor balanced each other in this situation, so he waited, and Joseph followed suit.

After about 15 minutes the disabled float unceremoniously ended in a side ditch and the parade resumed. Eric thought this might work out better after all. He slipped to the edge of the crowd, pretending to adjust his outfit. As he passed the doorway, the door opened and two men stepped out to watch the parade. *Oops, plan just disintegrated.*

As Eric walked past his intended entrance, he gave Joseph a sign to continue with the plan. When Joseph came to his doorway, he stepped aside to adjust his outfit. No one seemed to notice. Eric waited until he had reached the building's edge, then he slipped to the door on the east side near the collapsed fire escape. He was now out of direct sight of the parade. He paused, pretending to adjust his clown suit. Again, no one paid attention. While Eric went through this motion, a man suddenly opened the door and started to walk past Eric.

The bulge in the man's coat clearly showed he was carrying a pistol. *One of the Arkwell guards!* As the guard passed, Eric turned and dealt a heavy blow to the back of the man's head. He collapsed into Eric's arms. Eric dragged him to the other side of the fire escape, out of view of the throng. The guard remained unconscious while Eric bound, gagged, and cuffed him to the rusty metal framework.

Eric entered the open door and looked around. *Nobody in sight.* Then he ran down the hallway to the door where Joseph was waiting on the other side. Joseph was surprised to see Eric, but Eric's gestures briefly told the story.

Their first goal accomplished, they now must find the hostages and, if necessary, disarm guards. If the two guards outside decided to return, Joseph and Eric would need to do whatever they could to disable them. Maybe the guards would stay outside to watch the parade. It might go on for at least another hour.

Eric and Joseph did a quick search of the first floor, but found nothing. On the second floor they found nothing. The same for the third floor. On the fourth floor they saw a guard staring out a window, preoccupied with the parade. Joseph clobbered him with one of his patented hooks and the man fell unconscious to the floor. After they cuffed and gagged him, they searched the floor for hostages. They found no one. Surely the hostages will be on the fifth floor, they thought, racing up a flight of stairs. No one home there either. *Have we fallen for a trap?*

An additional frustration was that Sarah's transmitter had not sent signals during their search. Had the battery run down? Or had the guards found her unit and disabled it? Puzzled, they remembered that old buildings often sported roof-top storage rooms. They found a ladder leading to the roof, and, squinting into the sun, located a small, locked room.

They easily removed the lock with a tool, pushed open the door and found Sarah, Devon and Fran bound hand and foot. They sat wide-eyed and grateful to see two clowns; anybody but the thugs who had abducted them was a welcome sight.

"Ready for a disappearing act?" Eric said. Immediately the clowns began releasing their bonds.

"Eric! Where have you been?" quipped Sarah, once she regained composure. She still had a sense of humor even after an awful ordeal. Once released, the three captives hugged Eric and Joseph. Cautiously, they made their way to the first floor and out the door by the fire escape, where the unconscious guard still lay.

"No use disturbing the two gawking guards at the front of the building," Eric said. "Let them find their companions and guess what happened!"

Clown suits cast off, they hustled everyone into Eric's pickup. Using back streets to avoid the blocked off parade route, they drove rapidly away from the hostage site. Joseph said, "I would like to see the facial expressions on the two parade-watching guards when they go back inside. At least an hour might pass before they find their bound friends."

Eric called the local sheriff and suggested it might be a good time to use a warrant to catch the four guards at kidnap hotel. The law would have easy access to the building, because, before they left, Joseph and Eric had disabled locks on all the outer doors except the front door by the distracted guards. Eric then called authorities so they could make good use of warrants to arrest Arkwell Oil executives before the crooks discovered that their plan had failed.

Relieved to have rescued his friends, Eric anxiously waited to turn over all the evidence he had accumulated on Arkwell Oil and associates. *Let the professionals handle it from here on. I just want to resolve this case. I am tired of chasing from farm to city, from country to country, rescuing my fiancée . . . oops . . . I mean my friends!* He smiled. Then Eric nodded, glad that at last the crooks would be in jail for a good long time.

They returned to Devon and Fran's house, where they worked together to put things back in order. Eric thanked everyone for helping crack the case. He assured them that Arkwell Oil would be defunct in no time. He anticipated that many arrests would follow.

They all went out for a celebration dinner, and each former hostage told her or his version of the kidnapping. They all laughed at the clown rescue. What a wonderful evening. At last the case was closed.

As dessert arrived, Eric's cell phone went off. He answered good-naturedly, "Hello, this is Eric."

"Eric, this is Colonel French, Director of the Arkansas State Police. I have some mixed news."

Eric stopped smiling. "What is it?"

"By the time we got our legal clearances arranged and our folk arrived at Arkwell Oil Company headquarters and Sarah's farm . . . you may not believe this but . . . ."

"Go on," Eric felt a knot in his stomach growing tighter by the second.

"None of the executives were there . . . at either place. We found a few roughnecks milling around, very confused. They said a company rep suddenly ran to his car and roared away. At Arkwell's headquarters, only a few secretarial staff remained. They also acted bewildered and said that their bosses grabbed some files and fled after receiving a call."

Eric let the phone sag away from his ear, although the Director kept talking. "Eric, I have never seen anything like this. We have APBs out for all the names the roughnecks and secretaries provided us. The addresses where these people supposedly live are either fictitious or vacant. Looks like this is a group with a predesigned escape plan for all guilty parties. I also had a call from an Officer Wilson with the Little Rock police, Precinct 2. He reported that his captain also vanished."

Eric's jaw dropped to the floor. At last he thanked the Director and fell into a chair, staring at nothing in particular.

"Eric! What's the matter?" Sarah asked anxiously.

Eric tried to regain his composure. Slowly he repeated what the state official had told him. "I have never heard of such a well-arranged escape plan. These guys would make Houdini look like an amateur. The two guards must have gone inside, found the bound guards, and called Arkwell's headquarters before they could be intercepted."

Joseph spoke up, "I have an idea where they might be or at least where the dumbest ones are."

"Where?" demanded Eric.

"Auxolo, of course. It is the perfect place to disappear. Then they can return later and set up another scheme."

"Yes! A perfect escape location, if they don't know about the raid."

"I think these guys were alerted about our clown rescue, but I doubt they knew about our little raid in Mexico," Joseph said. "A quick visit to Auxolo might catch some bad guys."

Eric thought a moment and wondered if state and federal authorities should take it from here. Then he shook his head. If a U.S. government agency tried to catch and extradite those people, all sorts of problems might pop up. Politics and jurisdiction would be issues. And what would prevent the bad guys from leapfrogging to another remote area? Plus, going through normal channels would take too long. *No. The net might have too many holes in it to catch the real culprits.*

Eric sighed and looked at Joseph who nodded with a wry grin. "I agree," said Joseph, recognizing Eric's expression. "Shall we pack our bags? If we hurry we might get there before they figure out what happened to the roughnecks and guards at Auxolo."

Chapter 26

This time another passenger rode with them, Officer Craig Wilson. Wilson said, "That crooked captain needs to be caught and I need to be there." Wilson wore plain clothes.

Eric replied, "I'm glad for a third person. There will be a large number of criminals, and most of them may be armed."

When Eric and Joseph passed through customs again after only a few days, this time with a police officer, other phone calls by Eric to state officials and the FBI made the crossing barely possible. Many questions were asked but eventually they passed into Mexico. After all, this might be a wild goose chase, if the Arkwell people had already discovered that no one was at the Auxolo site. Eric's friend at the FBI was skeptical but agreed to stay in the background until the fugitives were captured and delivered at the border.

Of course, Eric's contact in Mexico provided the necessary weaponry for the trio. Wilson was impressed with Eric's connections but kept his thoughts to himself.

Joseph and Eric knew the Mexican roads by now and bypassed the hermit with his high-powered rifle. He could have his solitude; they would not disturb him. Joseph hoped the Arkwell escapees would use the slower route through the hermit's territory. He might detain them long enough for the rescuers to arrive in time.

Things went a little faster than on their first visit, but they still had to camp out in the mountains. The pickup bed was crowded with three men, but it kept off snakes and various carnivores. Finally, they bounced the last few hours to the Auxolo River site.

How close would they be able to get to the mine without being detected? How about guards? Or, and this made everyone uneasy, suppose the site was abandoned with no trace of another destination? Eric and Joseph silently agreed they would have no clue where to look next if Auxolo turned up dry.

Within a half mile of the quarry, Eric stopped the pickup and the men started their walk to uncertainty. Nearing the mine area, the familiar crack of a rifle greeted them. A bullet whined and kicked up dust and rocks to their left. Eric hit the ground, grumbling, "Been there, done that! At least the site is occupied."

Joseph wryly commented, "Looks like they don't want to give up easily."

Eric sighed, "Well, we know where they are. Now all we have to do is catch them! Unfortunately, it won't be by surprise." The trio crawled to the safety of a small mound and peered out. A bullet disturbed dust nearby.

"He's on the next mound, fairly well exposed," Eric said. "I think I can get a shot off." As he positioned his rifle, a second sniper bullet missed him. Eric raised up just enough to sight, then he pulled the trigger. Someone screamed.

"Let's move—but be careful," Eric urged. The assault team scrambled to the next depression and waited. Nothing. No more gunfire spoke to them. Instead, they heard the whirl of a pickup engine being started and then the sound of wheels spinning on gravel.

"Let's go!" said Eric. They reached the spot where the guard had fallen.

Joseph looked at the man. "He's not dead—just out cold. Your shot grazed his skull. The wound is not fatal."

"Good," said Eric, glad the man would live.

Looking over to the next mound, they saw a pickup dashing out of the valley and heading up the mountainside. In full view of Eric and his team, seven men ran toward pickup trucks. Eric fired a shot in the air and shouted for them to stop. As if suddenly frozen, the fleeing men stopped cold and held their hands over their heads.

Eric spoke, "Is one of you Murphy Edwards?"

Several of the captives pointed to the departing vehicle. One of them said, "He's the driver."

"Who's with him?"

"Edwin McCloskey, Spencer Frye, Frank Zietel, and the cop. They ditched us."

So, the company's top guns panicked. It must be every man for himself as the posse closes in. How classic!

Then, like an audience watching drama unfold in a theater, the gang of seven, along with Eric's team, watched Edwards' pickup bounce wildly up the mountain slope. The driver lost control and the vehicle spun sideways, careening toward a steep cliff. As the pickup started to turn over, it sideswiped an outcrop of quartzite. Sparks flew. The tough rock slashed open the gas tank and fuel immediately ignited. The pickup rolled over and over down the slope, flames enveloping it. A fireball blocked the view of the shocked watchers.

Eric turned to his companions. "They knew if caught and convicted of murder, none of them would ever see anything again but the inside of a prison, or worse." Glumly he said, "What a horrible death."

The seven remaining Arkwell employees were lesser offenders, if such a thing is possible. Perhaps they were actually smarter than the five dead ones. Better to take their chances in the courts, plead guilty, and hope for life after prison.

The Arkwell people cleaned up the quarry site, buried the charred remains, and bandaged the wounded guard.

"Let's get out of here," Eric said. "I've had enough of Auxolo. I don't ever want to see this place again." Joseph and Wilson nodded in agreement.

The Arkwell employees received a private escort across the Mexican landscape. This time, after returning the guns and leaving the guards' weapons with Eric's friend, they drove to the border. There was extensive questioning and only Eric's many connections with the FBI and state made the crossing possible. State and federal law officials shared the glory of taking the crooks into custody.

On returning to Little Rock, Officer Wilson shook hands with Joseph and Eric. "This is the best thing that's happened in my ten years on the force. Thanks for letting me go along."

"None of this could have been done without your careful work going over police reports and files," said Eric.

At last it was over.

Chapter 27

*A*fter Wilson left to rejoin his family, Eric said, "Joseph, I don't know what I would have done without you and your undercover work. You are such a creative, helpful, and loyal person."

Joseph blushed at the praise. He said, "I just cannot stand to see bad stuff get by. It was an honor to work with you, Eric. I did not know private investigators had so much fun." They both laughed.

Eric became serious. "Joseph, my private investigation business is busier than I ever thought it would be. Word of what's been going on has spread, and Megan says at least a dozen projects are calling my name. My geological consulting business is picking up, too. I can't handle all this. Would you join my business as a partner?"

Joseph eyes flew open with shock. "I . . . I . . . don't know what to say. I guess . . . I guess that would be all right. I think I am ready for a change. I'll need to call Sophia in California to get her OK. She will be back soon."

"Great! You start tomorrow!"

Joseph stood processing the offer as Eric dashed to his pickup and drove off to visit Sarah. Eric called over his shoulder, "I'll catch up with you at the office in the morning. See you!"

Joseph watched as Eric's pickup sped off. *What have I agreed to?* He shook his head and called his wife. Sophia's month-long visit to relatives in California was about to end. She had been worried with the dangers Joseph faced. Each day, Joseph had texted Sophia to assure her that he was okay. She was surprised at the offer and asked Joseph if the job was always so dangerous. He told her that most things Eric was involved with were rather mild. She should not worry. Joseph hoped he was forecasting the future correctly. If only he knew!

Eric needed to talk with Sarah. He had called her at work and asked when she thought she'd be home. Sarah said she would leave immediately; Stan would understand. As Eric drove to the farm, he could see her in his imagination, beautiful as usual.

Sarah was waiting for him on the front porch. He had barely turned off the engine when she came running toward him. She fairly leaped into his arms, smothering him with kisses.

Eric managed to get a few words out during her barrage of affection. "Sarah I . . . we . . . should talk."

She led him through the front door and into the living room, where she pulled him to the sofa. She wrapped her arms around his neck and pulled him close. Eric enjoyed the embrace for a few moments. Then he managed to gently disentangle himself from her clinging arms. "Sarah . . . we need to talk."

Sarah felt rebuffed and made a pouty face.

"Sarah, this whole business is wrapping up. We promised to talk once it was over."

"Yes, yes!" she said excitedly.

Eric stood and suggested they go to the kitchen. "How about we talk over a cup of coffee? I love your coffee."

Sarah jumped up and ran to the kitchen. Wanting to speed up the conversation, she quickly grabbed the coffee maker and coffee. Eric waited at the kitchen table opposite her chair. She noticed this but thought little of it. While the coffee brewed, she scrambled for some cookies. After what seemed like an eternity, the coffee was ready and she brought steaming cups to the table.

"So let's talk," she said, her hazel eyes bright. Eric looked into those beautiful eyes and found it difficult to speak. He wanted to express his affection for Sarah, but he didn't know how to begin. Finally he cleared his throat and plunged in.

"Sarah, you are the only woman I have ever dated whom I have felt comfortable around. You are a wonderful person, a spiritual person, and a brave person."

She smiled at these accolades. "And you are the most amazing man I ever met," she replied with enthusiasm. "You have such strength of character and are so thoughtful, kind, and . . . ."

Eric cut her list short. "'We really need to talk about where we are now and what we should do from here on."

Sarah shyly pointed to the sofa and laughed. Eric felt as she did but wrestled with himself to continue.

"Sarah, please follow my thoughts. I feel we should take some time to get to know each other and find out who we really are. Look at how long we have known each other; it's been only a brief moment and most of it is connected to the excitement of the investigation."

Sarah's face turned serious. "Eric, what are you saying?"

"I'm just saying we need time to learn about each other. I barely know you and I think you hardly know me."

Sarah's voice almost cracked, "But I thought . . . ." Her words trailed off and her eyes became sad.

Eric rushed to repair the damage and took her hands in his. "Sarah, please know that I care a great deal for you . . . don't get me wrong. But we need to make sure our relationship isn't just about passion and a case that drew us together; it will take more than that to make us a happy couple. Do you see my point?"

Sarah reluctantly nodded her head, although her eyes were on the verge of tears. "What . . . what do you suggest?" Her voice quivered.

"All I'm saying is that we should start slowly . . . sort of begin with casual dating so we can get to know each other. I know that may not sound very exciting, but anything worth having is worth the effort to make it work well."

Sarah sighed deeply and the well of tears did not overflow. Truthfully, with the closing of the case, she too had begun to wonder what to do next. *Should I order a wedding gown or back off and rethink my life? I am a single woman with no immediate family, so I must be careful. I need to make decisions that will work toward the life I really want . . . whatever that is.*

She sat a little straighter in her chair and spoke in a more collected voice, "I understand what you are saying, Eric. I agree we both need to reevaluate our relationship."

Eric breathed a sigh of relief and finished off his coffee. He reached for a cookie and broke it in two. "We need to close this case, Sarah. Are you ready?"

"Yes," Sarah said. "Where are we, anyway?"

Eric pulled out sworn statements from employees of Arkwell Oil. "From what these folks have said, we have a clear idea of Bodien Kessel's place in the whole operation. He was the muscle man involved in nabbing roughnecks who became suspicious about what was being pumped into the fake oil wells. Others in the gang drugged the roughnecks and smuggled them into Mexico where they became slave laborers in the zinc mine.

"According to multiple employees, Bodien pushed Danny to his death. Bodien had managed to get to the crow's nest while Danny was working there. He was on the tower and Danny couldn't see him because of the bright lights. Then Bodien cut the harness low from the back and shoved Danny all in one motion. That made Danny's scream understandable: 'Not that! Nooo!' And the burn on the side of his face came from slipping out of the harness.

"One of the supervisors arranged for Bodien to escape while everyone attended to Danny. Danny was killed because he told his supervisor he saw toxic waste being pumped into a completed well. He intended to go to the police with this information the next day. That sealed his fate."

Sarah nodded as Eric spoke.

"Since you are his sister, they couldn't risk him escaping a kidnapping attempt. That would bring down the company. So they hired Bodien to do the dirty work."

Sarah stared at the kitchen wall for a long moment before she said, "Please go on."

"Bodien took the harness with him when he made his escape. He gave it to McCleaver, the guy I shot at your home. McCleaver then gave it to another gang member, who was supposed to destroy it. That was a major error that sabotaged the plan. The guy figured he could make a little extra money by taking it to Frankie, the recycler. That greedy mistake eventually brought down the company. It is the little things that matter.

"As far as why Bodien was killed, it's clear that his fatal error was to irritate Jean. She is not someone who takes kindly to threats.

"The missing roughnecks are all alive and accounted for. The lesser staff we brought back from Mexico blame the top four in the company for decisions to run Arkwell Oil as a criminal operation. The police captain was key to the plan's success since he could intercept complaints and bury problems so that nothing went past his desk. The top guys and the captain lost their lives trying to escape. I feel sorry for people who think they need to go outside the law to get what they want from life. I feel even more sorrow for those who cannot stand up to what they have done and admit their wrongs.

"My heart goes out to deceased persons in this case. I pray for their family members. That I am involved, directly and indirectly in some of the deaths, is a heavy weight on my conscience. I'm planning to see my pastor to help me work through the sorrow I have about shooting people."

Sarah listened intently as Eric spoke. Although her brother had died tragically, she was proud of him for taking a stand to do the right thing. "Eric, thank you for all you did to bring this case to closure. How terrible it would be if this criminal activity kept going. My brother was such a brave person . . . ." She couldn't finish the thought.

Coming to her rescue, Eric said, "Sarah, thanks for hiring me to investigate Danny's fall. Without your desire for an explanation, things would not have gone as they did. You deserve huge credit for bringing down Arkwell Oil."

Smiling grimly, Sarah nodded. Then she asked about her former friend, Jean. Sarah was deeply troubled that Jean had entered the criminal world as an assassin.

"The sheriff told me that Jean confessed to everything and implicated the deceased Murphy Edwards. The thugs in the hospital are out of their comas. They too have confessed, along with those in jail. Edwards was the contact man who arranged for kidnapping and killing. Apparently, he went into hiding and worked behind the scenes after he disappeared from his office."

"Why would Jean get mixed up in that awful affair? I considered her a friend."

"I wish I knew why people choose to do bad things, Sarah. Jean will have to face a court of law and pay for her decisions, as well as all the guilty parties associated with Arkwell Oil."

After a pause in the conversation, Sarah and Eric looked at each other. He broke the ice. "This whole investigation has been amazing. I'd like to offer a prayer of thankfulness."

Sarah agreed. Eric offered thanks for safety and for stopping an awful criminal operation. Sarah said, "Amen!" and gave a relieved sigh.

Eric looked at her thoughtfully. He did not want to leave her dangling with uncertainty about their relationship. "Sarah, may I take you to dinner Sunday after church? Are you free?"

"Eric, I'd be delighted," Sarah replied with a smile. The invitation felt formal, but she understood his method.

They parted by squeezing hands. Sarah watched him go to his pickup. She waved as he pulled away; Eric waved back. Then she went to her bedroom, sprawled on her bed, and burst into tears. They were not tears of loss, but tears released from a myriad of emotions. The stress and pressure of the last few weeks cascaded out in great volumes. She needed to let it all out. Tears have many purposes, and now she was experiencing them.

Tucked inside those emotions was hope. It was a hope that the wonderful man she had hired to do a job might turn out to be more than an employee. At this she smiled inwardly. Eventually, the smile reached her lips and a broad grin mingled with residual tears. *Yes, the future does hold many hopes, and one of those hopes has a name: Eric Bonfield.*

Eric drove slowly back to town, his mind tugging a dozen different ways. Sarah occupied several of those tugs. *Who is she to me? She began as my employer; then she became someone I protected with my life, and now she is a romantic partner. It had happened so fast!*

He admitted to himself that he had feelings of fear. *But what am I afraid of? Sarah? Hardly. She has so many of the qualities I unconsciously want in a woman. She can't be the problem.*

Eric thought out loud, "If this was ten years ago, I'd be married by now! But I guess that maturity means I think more clearly about life's big decisions. And I want to take enough time with the decision about who I marry. Marry? Brrr! That sounds so scary. But I don't fear Sarah. She is ideal in so many ways. Yet, I know, from talking with Megan, that rose-colored glasses need to be removed. We must take our time."

Eric almost bit his lip before he continued talking to himself. "I only hope Sarah will wait." Then he smiled. He knew she would wait, and that waiting would make their final decision so much more delicious!

Eric also felt strange letting go of the investigation. Oh, he would testify in court many times in the future. Testimonies didn't concern him much; they went with the territory. He wanted to see justice served. But such a criminal scheme always leaves damage in its wake. The contaminated wells would need to be pumped as dry as possible. Toxic chemicals in neighboring water wells must be dealt with. Considering the many contaminated wells in the area, a massive cleanup will be involved.

Arkwell Oil would never drill another well. But what about the manufacturing companies that had paid Arkwell to dispose of their waste without a thought as to what happened to the noxious residues? They will face huge fines for their lack of environmental concern.

Whatever resources Arkwell owns will be confiscated and paid to those who have been harmed. But the cleanup will require far more resources than a small company can deliver. Eric shook his head. He was all too familiar with these cases. The state or federal governments will be left to pick up the tab. In the end, taxpayer money will pay the bill. *That isn't fair. I wish there was a way to prevent such things from happening.* Then his idealism and reality balanced themselves in his mind, and he realized that systems are what they are. *Criminals need to be stopped and that is where I find my entry point. My small piece of the world is all that I am responsible for, and I will do what I can.*

By the time Eric arrived at his office the next day, Joseph was already there, talking with Megan. Joseph beamed about his "desk job." Rubbing his shoulder, he laughed, "This sure beats running a wrench on the rig!" Then he saw his desk was piled with a stack of papers almost equal in height to the stack on Eric's desk. "Whoa!" he exclaimed. "Is all that mine?" Megan nodded and smiled.

Eric chuckled, "Well, Joseph, get to work! You never know what the next phone call will bring."

Just at that moment, the phone rang. Megan answered, listened for a minute, then turned to Eric and said, "It's for you. Don't take your boots off yet."

ABOUT THE AUTHOR

Max W. Reams, Ph.D., taught geology at Olivet Nazarene University, Bourbonnais, IL, for five decades. He is a Certified Life Coach, speaker, Trainer for Life Innovations, Inc., and author of *Geology of Illinois State Parks*.

32809064R00114